MW01519916

Several Women Dancing

Several Women Dancing

Paul Dutton

THE MERCURY PRESS

Copyright © 2002 by Paul Dutton

THIS IS A WORK OF FICTION and is not intended as a depiction
of actual events or of persons living or dead.

ALL RIGHTS RESERVED. No part of this book may be reproduced by any
means without the prior written permission of the publisher, with the exception
of brief passages in reviews. Any request for photocopying or other reprographic
copying of any part of this book must be directed in writing to the Canadian
Reprography Collective.

The publisher gratefully acknowledges the financial assistance of the Canada
Council for the Arts, the Ontario Arts Council, and the Ontario Tax Credit
Program. The publisher further acknowledges the financial support of the
Government of Canada through the Department of Canadian Heritage's Book
Publishing Industry Development Program (BPIDP) for our publishing activities.

SECTIONS of this novel have been previously published in *Rampike*, *Descant*,
and *Sex: An Anthology* (The Mercury Press, 2001).

THE AUTHOR is grateful for support provided for the writing of this
book through grants from The Canada Council for the Arts, the Ontario Arts
Council (Writers' Reserve Program), and the Toronto Arts Council.

Edited by Beverley Daurio
Copy-edited by Stuart Ross
Cover design by Gordon Robertson
Composition and page design by Beverley Daurio

Printed and bound in Canada
Printed on acid-free paper

1 2 3 4 5   06 05 04 03 02

Canadian Cataloguing in Publication Data
Dutton, Paul, 1943–
Several women dancing / Paul Dutton.
ISBN 1-55128-096-5
I. Title.
PS8557.U88S48 2002   C813'.54   C2002-904584-3
PR9199.3.D89S48 2002

The Mercury Press
Box 672, Station P, Toronto, Ontario Canada M4S 2Y4
www.themercurypress.ca

This book is dedicated to several women—Helen Weinzweig, Mari-Lou Rowley, Anne Michaels, Adele Wiseman, and Myra Fried—who encouraged and sustained its writing, and to the many others who inspired it.

What's lovely
is whatever makes the adrenalin run;
therefore I count terror and fear among
the greatest beauty. The greatest
beauty is to be alive, forgetting nothing,
although remembrance hurts
like a foolish act, is a foolish act.

— *John Newlove, "The Double-Headed Snake"*

1

I can remember exactly when the obsession began, a minor
feature distinguishing it from the many other obsessions I have
undergone with young and beautiful women, though far from
the only distinguishing feature of this particular, this most tena-
cious, this most perilously consuming of the innumerable such
obsessions I've fallen prey to over the course of my solitary existence, so riven with senseless fascinations, futile fallings-in-love,
hopeless hangings-of-the-heart upon patently unobtainable
objects of affection or, perhaps more properly, lust or, even
more accurately and darkly, some unnameable—or at any rate,
unnamed—passion, instinct, or perversion, all the more powerful for being compulsive, dangerous, obscure. I can remember exactly. She appeared in an abbreviated version of the
black-and-white garb associated with a French maid: little
white cap, black high-heeled shoes, black stockings, frilled
black garter belt, black panties, tiny black apron fringed with
lacy white, its black bow around her waist, holding the body
of it to her belly, the broad straps, secured at the nape of her

neck by another bow, loosely permitting the free and fluid movement of her breasts—her perfect, soft breasts, neither too ample nor too spare, that flirted tauntingly (now on view, now obscured) round the straps of the apron; with a smile playing constantly over her face within the dark fringe of her hair, parted in the middle, brushing, when she leant her head to one side, the soft white flesh of her shoulder, as she danced for the pleasure of the roomful of men in the yearning, masturbatory darkness of the strip club, whose depths, or perhaps I should say lengths, for it is a long and narrow room, the stage down one side, with four rows of seats facing it, the rows divided by a brief aisle into which juts a small extension of the stage, which extension, were it longer, would be termed a runway, and with other rows of seats, largely unoccupied, ranked back from either end of the stage...as she danced for the pleasure of the roomful of men in the yearning, masturbatory darkness of the strip club, whose depths, or lengths, I had repaired to, now, as so often, out of a sense of burning urgency, and felt, as I drank in her every move with rapt gaze, that this time, this one momentous evening, or afternoon, or whatever it was, my abandonment of incidental, though not unimportant, under-takings and my hastening to this fusty den, had occurred in response to, not a prurient whim, but a deep elemental call, an unconscious signal transmitted from somewhere within the depths of her on a frequency only I could receive, a signal that cut through the pervasive static characterizing my day-to-day existence and that drew me, with siren magnetism, to the dark room with the stage lit, where she appeared in her brief black costume and smiled as her nakedness promised itself, and her hair, cut just below her shoulders, flipped round the flashing white of her flesh, and my cock sprang immediately to attention, my eyes lusting for the swift disclosure of her physical secrets, a lust fulfilled before the first song she danced to was finished, the slight black panties deftly removed and my heart racing at the view of her genitals so generously afforded me. I remember exactly: her close-cropped hair, her dark flesh, her leather apparel, her frowning demeanour, the long, futile wait for the G-string to be dispensed with, the aching disappointment at never seeing her soft pubic area, wondering why she would not reveal that most intimate of her physical charms, as she beckoned me close, with crook'd finger and teasing voice, from where I stood retiring in the black obscurity of the standing section behind the four rows of wide-eyed spectators. Her eyes. They were dark brown, lit with delight in the pleasure she implied with her spread legs and the moist slit of her vulva, as she lifted her left leg to accept, in the top of the black stocking that adorned her right leg, the votive dollar or two-dollar bill from the lucky patron in the front row who thereby gained a closer view of the dark, curled hairs and soft, pink lips of her (what I called then, in the heat of romantic inflammation) seat of satisfaction—*Introibo ad altare deae*, the goddess who gives joy to the throbbing tumescence of my manhood; *Confiteor Deo omnipotenti, beatae Mariae semper virgini, beato Michaeli Archangelo, beato Johanni Baptistae, sanctis apostolis, Petro et Paulo, omnibus sanctis, et tibi, Pater, quia peccavi nimis cogitatione, verbo et operae, mea culpa, mea culpa, mea maxima culpa,* I confess that I would approach the altar of the goddess who might give joy to my vanishing youth, through my fault, through my fault, through my most grievous fault, through my failing vision and sight-aiding spectacles, oh what a spectacle she presents to my burning eyes in the anonymous gloom of the secretive strip club, as the apron strap slips from her shoulder to free her breast to unrestricted view, and the other strap and the other breast and the bow at the back, and the apron is gone and all that conceals her last bits of flesh are the transparent stockings and slender garter belt, which she never removes, as she pulses and rocks to the sensual rhythms, grinding her crotch and spreading her buttocks to please the hungry, collective eye of the straining, insatiable gathering of men.

And what eye more hungry, more insatiable than mine, unless it be all of them taken together? For an Alps of desire arises within me, a range of arousal whose peaks protrude into each succeeding day's efforts at work, through every night's drowse into slumber, through any attempt I make to fulfill my lust with one of the easy pickups encountered at party or bar, no matter the effort expended to thrust from my mind the image of her, to expel the conviction that none but she can answer the drive that consumes me—she, in the supremacy of her womanhood, the arch and utter, supple physical feminacy she possesses. Oh, I fought it. I fought it and thought I'd beaten it, lectured myself interminably, catalogued the innumerable cases of similar sort that had plagued me over the years, resisted the urge to return again, during those weeks when a call to the strip club assured me that she was appearing, to return and witness again, in the flesh, the images my mind's eye would not surrender. But more. I found myself scheming to do more than just watch her, devising a means to make her want to meet me, something beyond the crude advances she doubtlessly daily endured, something to make her realize the earnestness, the respect with which I wished to approach her, something refined, something dignified. Flowers. During one of the weeks when I knew she was on at the club, I would purchase some flowers—nothing cheap, nothing trite, but rather, an impressive bouquet, roses perhaps, long-stemmed, something to let her know I wasn't being whimsical; delivered to her at, of course, the club (knowing nowhere else to send them), with a note: "From a secret admirer." I imagined the flurry the bouquet's arrival would spark among the other dancers, the offhand manner in which she would treat the event, but the private delight she would nurture, without ever conveying it to the coarsely cracking bits of fluff around her, who would speculate on who wanted into her pants, what classy guy was preparing to brighten the sordid world she lived in, of pawing patrons and demanding club owners. And then a second bouquet, with, this time, the note saying, "From a secret admirer who wishes to meet you." And a third: "Tonight, last seat, last row, by the dressing room, after your final performance." And her curiosity would be caught. No. Not just her curiosity. Her spirit of romance, of adventure. Her desire to be treated as more than a hunk of flesh. And she meets me, saying, "Hi, Secret. What have you got in mind?" and smiles in a warm and delighted manner, tugging on my arm as I stand, mildly a-flutter, solicitous, expressing my pleasure at her acceptance of my invitation, as she pulls me along, saying, "Come on, where are you taking me, Mr. Admirer?" holding the latest bouquet of flowers, laughing a little, amused and intrigued, smiling as we walk the length of the club by the back row of seats, through the knot of men standing there during the last stripper's dance, descending the stairs and chatting, exchanging names (her real name, not her stage name), passing through the crowds on the main street to my car, in which I whisk her away to someplace classy, a piano bar I know in a ritzy hotel, and it's easy to tell she's taken by me, by my wit, my urbanity, my easy, gentle, sensitive manner, and I by her, by her intelligence, humour, warmth, beauty, femininity; so that, quite naturally, ineluctably, we find ourselves at her apartment door and she is inviting me in for a nightcap—Courvoisier—during which, at one point, she drops her head back on the cushion of the sofa we share and sighs through slightly opened lips, then runs her tongue softly over them, leaving them glistening, her eyes closed, the invitation obvious, letting me press my lips to hers in a kiss that begins gently, tentatively, gradually building, in a crescendo of passion, to a gasping, moaning fever of open mouths, flicking tongues, and biting teeth, from which suddenly she breaks, pushing me back, forcing herself from my embrace, to disappear in silence and leave me disconsolate, apprehensive now, as seconds meld into minutes, fearful that she will not return, or worse, that someone else will appear, a man perhaps, to wreak unspeakable vengeance, beat and rob me, to—but no, because now, from the bedroom door, in the dim light, she emerges and—god of gods, lord of Jesus lord, Christ almighty, I can't believe it—she's wearing the costume I first saw her in and is smiling and moves without music through the tantalizing choreography I would never, in my wildest imaginings, have believed she might someday perform for my exclusive pleasure, but which she does, to the sole accompaniment of my mounting desire, her naked beauty just inches away, as, clad only in stockings and garter belt now, she slowly, teasingly, removes my clothing and leads me then to her sumptuous bed, indulging with me there in every manner of mutual sexual satisfaction that two people are capable of.

I refrained from sending the flowers, knowing it would lead nowhere, or to embarrassment, humiliation, as I sat in the last seat, last row, by the dressing room, after her final performance, where she would approach me with her burly boyfriend, who would say, "You de guy dat's been sendin' my girl flowers? Come on wid us. *Bot'* of us!" the angry questions, the accusations, protestations on my part, pleading finally, in the dark alley back of the strip club to which he had silently forced me to exit, out the back door, no escape, no chance to flee through the teeming streets, unseen, unremembered, never to return to the dark and dangerous interior from whose perilous reaches I had so barely managed to secure my freedom, living for days in continual panic at the possibility that he may have followed me, traced me, in some way found me out or chanced upon me, now to administer the punishment I had so luckily eluded, a brute beyond reasoning with, a pathological sadist intent on mangling me for the sheer fun of it, all under the guise of redressing the sullied honour of his offended mate, his sweet and innocent Maria or Teresa or Jenny or Debra, who only went into this line of work out of desperation or dreams of stardom in some more serious, at least more respectable area of the entertainment world, settling for a temporary, distasteful means of earning a living until her big break came and she could enjoy the fame and fortune she was so obviously meant for. I refrained from sending them, I refrained from going myself, I refrained from calling to discover if she were appearing there, I wiped her from my mind, I obliterated, with steely resolve, the least hint of any impulse to even dwell on her memory. I congratulated myself. I had won. I was not obsessed. I would not be obsessed. It was over. The slightest twinge of regret or desire was doused with a torrent of reason, maturity, common sense.

Months passed. No change. That's it. Done.

2

I guess it was a few months later that the ad with her picture appeared in the morning tabloid and I left work early for a doctor's appointment to drive to the suburban bar where the ad informed me she was appearing. I can't remember what led me to leaf through the sleazy rag that carried news of who was where on the strip-bar circuit, but I do remember the picture. "Also this week JULIE," the ad proclaimed, with the picture of an awfully cheap-looking Julie in a dress that came down to her hips and continued only behind her, revealing legs that were meant to be enticing but that left me cold, the coals of my passion fired only by the incendiary representation of the majestic **BLACK SATIN**—her name in large, bold capitals, her likeness reproduced beneath in alluring sensuality, her supple form sparsely clothed in metal-studded black leather, a whip stretched taut from her left hand—which held, close to her breast, between thumb and forefinger, the several strands of braided leather—to her right hand, which extended beyond her body and held...well, here the offensive Julie intervened with her repugnant inset, but I assume that the hidden right hand held the butt end of the whip with beguiling grace. Her neck was encircled by a studded leather collar. A leather halter with full-length sleeves dipped down from her shoulders to partially cover each breast, a leather thong laced through metal eyelets on either side of its open front, crisscrossing her half-exposed bosom. Round her midriff, a leather strap with eight metal studs extended over each hip into leather leggings, cut away in front to expose the soft flesh of her lower abdomen, the gentle swell of her dark-tufted mound and pink vulva concealed by a studded leather G-string.

I found myself at a stage-side table, with a beer in front of me and a cigarette in my hand. I endured one or two insipid disrobers before discovering myself in need of evacuatory relief. The men's washroom was downstairs at the end of a long corridor, with a shorter corridor giving off it to the right, where a pay phone was situated; and there, at the pay phone, in a black kimono with Chinese-dragon design, stood Black Satin, pensive and intent, head bent forward in earnest mien, the finger of her right hand tracing invisible doodles on the Formica shelf below the phone, bare legs visible from where the kimono ended, just above her knees, to the heels of her delicate feet, set in high-heeled slippers with tiny straps across the well-pedicured toes highlighted with red nail polish. I caught the words "If that's the way you feel." Inside the lavatory, I lingered at the urinal, listening for indications from outside that she'd completed her call. I washed my hands several times; resorted to combing my hair when someone else entered, so I wouldn't appear to be loitering; washed my hands yet again as I waited for him to leave; and finally, hearing the phone being hung up, exited, only to find the corridor empty. I returned to the john, praying that no one would enter, and after seconds of eternity, heard the clack of high heels and thrust myself into the corridor, at last to stand face to face with the woman I desired beyond all else. "Uh," I said, "er...um...uh..." Oh, the poetry my soul yearned to pour out to her, the suave, sophisticated phrases I had dreamt of enchanting her with, the smooth, intriguing remarks I had meant to endear her by, the "Excuse me, c-c-could I—" that I finally managed to stammer out, to which she responded with a patient, inquisitive "Yes?" "I—I...I wondered," I said, "I— uhm...uhhh...er—d-do you dance here often?" "I finish here this week. I don't know when I'll be back," she replied. The kimono hung loosely from her shoulders, open at the front. She wore a bra that was not a bra, but merely a thin strand of black material across the bottom of her breasts, lifting them slightly and causing them to protrude even more than they already did. A thin gold chain was strung about her waist. Panties of black silk-like material completed her ensemble. "I—uhn—I see," I said. "Mmm...uhhh...w-where will you be next week?" "At the Barbados, downtown." "Oooh," I responded, in a tone that revealed me to be, I hoped, duly impressed. "A...uh...nice place?" I inquired. "A place," she replied. "Welll...uhnn...have a good show." "Thank you," she said, and proceeded down the corridor, ascending the stairs to the main club as I followed silently at a respectful distance.

Upstairs she stood kimono-less, almost naked, in easy conversation with some men at a table by the bar, laughing and chatting as she waited for the interlude music to end and the tape to which she would dance to begin. I resumed my seat, trembling with passion, adopting an attitude of aloof superiority to the unseemly surroundings to which my obsession had driven me—at least, that's how I recollect the matter, though my memory is not that clear, in fact I think I fidgeted a lot, perhaps took nervous drags on my cigarette, sipped or gulped beer without pouring it into the glass provided, drinking quickly, I guess, although no, I believe I did sip from the glass, smoked languidly, my manner disinterested, my eyes seldom wandering from the beer bottle, the glass, the ashtray, the cigarette, the shiny Formica surface of the table—in brief, the immediate and tangible environment that impinged on my senses, all else a matter of indifference to me, no heed paid to the laughter with which she responded to the conversation of the men by whose table she stood, no notice taken by me of the whiteness of her flesh caught in the dim lights beyond the darkened stage in the middle of the room, which stage erupts in bright illumination upon her arrival to the accompaniment of pulsing music, the rhythms of which she moves to in sensual allurement, her gaze fixed upon me, her eyes alert to my every expression, sensitive to the least indication on my part of approval of the erotic undulations she executes for my benefit, so eager is she to please me, captivated by me since our encounter in the corridor downstairs, her small talk with the men at that table before she came onstage just a cover-up for her preoccupation with me, to whom she beckons with the index finger of her right hand and, upon my approach to the edge of the stage, turns her body, holding my gaze with her eyes, looking at me over her shoulder as she presents, inches from my face, the soft, firm globes of her buttocks, and bends to expose her genital area within the slight black fabric of her

G-string, which she removes with elaborate slowness, pulling it tight into her crotch and playing it back and forth to stimulate her vulva, whose lips I stare at as they move with the action of the G-string, which finally now is removed and the full splendour of her cunt is before me, with all its fleshy folds and varied tones and coarse surrounding hair, and near it, the brown wrinkled aureole of her asshole, distended by her posture, even more as she lowers herself to the stage, never taking her eyes off me, and lifts her leg over my head and reclines on her buttocks before me, grinding her pelvis and staring at me, smiling, resting on her elbows, her hands kneading her breasts, her fingers teasing her nipples firm, the thin non-bra strap beneath the fleshy, undulating breasts, so large and pink-tipped, the gentle blonde strands of her long hair straying across them in wanton abandon, the plush swell of her hips, the soft wisps of fair-coloured hair around her pubes, the delicious musty smell as she pulled my head closer and pressed my mouth down upon the moist and inviting opening, her large thighs clenching my head, her heels drumming an ecstatic tattoo upon my back as the music began and I dropped my cigarette in anticipation of her arrival on the suddenly illuminated stage in the middle of the room, to which she ascended and began dancing in her scanty attire to the frenetic beat of a rock song, her black hair flipping about her expressionless face, her slender hips bumping and grinding as she moved with svelte grace on slim-thighed legs through the erotic choreography of simulated copulation, at one point hailing a patron on the other side of the room to approach the stage and stooping over to him, her slight breasts close to his face as she pressed and caressed them, backing off quickly, with tantalizing smile, to lie on the stage with her high-heeled slippers kicked off, her right leg raised, right hand at its ankle, pulling back to spread her crotch, which remained within the confines of the black G-string the law forbade her to remove, and the music ended and she left the stage never once having so much as glanced in my direction, let alone at me, though there was one point at which our eyes met and I sensed the spark of excitement she felt as I stared in lust at her moist genital slit, into which she had inserted one or two active fingers, bringing herself to climax in defiance of laws statutory, social, moral, and professional, her red pubic hair soaked with the juices her lust for me had caused to flow, for which she obviously felt no shame, leaving the stage with a smile of sweet satisfaction, rolling her nipples between her fingers and sighing contentedly, giving her auburn curls a casual flip that bespoke her disdain for conventional attitudes generally and, specifically, for any disapproval that moralists might direct against her actions.

I suppose it was about an hour before I felt sufficiently free of guilt at having let my hand wander, during Black Satin's performance, into my pocket and, within that enclosure, across my thigh and over to my tumescent penis, where, inspired by the energetic titillation to which I was exposed, it rubbed, first gently and gradually more firmly, the straining organ through which there was eventually released a tingling eruption of fluid—sufficiently free of guilt, I say, and dry of pant, to be able to venture out into the suburban night. Thank god it was winter and I had an overcoat to conceal my indiscretion. Or was it summer and I was subjected to the knowing smirks of the truck drivers and factory workers who populated the seamy joint? They couldn't mistake the white crust on my brown pants, which I was powerless to prevent them from seeing, having no parcel or bag or garment to casually carry in such a way as to protect from their view the obvious soiling of my garment. But no, surely I was wearing my white pants, into whose tones the flaking, dried semen would within the hour have blended, camouflaged convincingly, especially in the murky atmosphere of the club. Whatever the case, no one but me was aware of my surreptitious indulgence and besides, even if they were, what did it matter? After all, I was in line with a literary tradition, playing Leopold Bloom to Black Satin's Gerty MacDowell. I am, in fact, I believe, not mistaken in my perception that the actual date of the incident was precisely June 16 and the actual hour that of sunset or thereabouts. And, as it falls out, a fireworks display occurred in the vicinity within the span of my presence there—or at any rate a string of ladyfingers was set off by some youngster playing in the parking lot of the mall the club was situated in as I walked to my car, it being, I recall, close on the 24th of May holiday, if not precisely that day. At any rate, I left, having sat through a last hour of dancers as I waited for my pants to dry, one of the dancers proving to be the very Julie whose objectionable photograph had marred the image of my desire in the morning tabloid, a Julie who, I was dismayed to discover, evinced, despite my earnest efforts to forfend it, a robust and persistent erection from what I had hoped would have been my declining member. I left, nevertheless, without further incident, never, I was sure, to return to any such place again.

3

When she took the stage at the Barbados, a sleazy, downtown main-drag strip joint, I'd been waiting an hour in the centre of the row of chairs that lined the aisle across from the stage, which faced a mirrored wall behind me, with bench seats and tables set along its length, the stage occupying half the centre portion of the long, narrow room consecrated to the slow ritual disrobing and display of flesh by young women with varying ability to contort, excite, delight, cavort, arouse, amuse, and generally inspire the male spirit to coital urges that must evaporate into surreptitious masturbation, sink under cresting waves of drink, or find an outlet in trade with the fluid-hipped whores who sway on the street outside or flow through the smoky currents inside the Barbados, its stage an island near whose shore I wait to see, see, bathe my eyes in the tangible waters of her flesh, scant feet from the chair whose tufts of upholstery I picked at absentmindedly where it poked out from the worn edge of the smooth vinyl covering, which, with the scuffed metal frame, I would soon inch closer to the raised platform she danced on, leaning to approach still nearer the spread limbs and thrusting pelvis, the plump *w* (or *m*) of her buttocks that kissed the stage (or teased the ceiling) with gentle suggestive bounces, wishing the stage were my mouth instead of the smooth hardwood floor so unworthy of the sweet burden she offered, which could be much more pleasurably—for her and for me—borne by the softer, more stimulating platform of my lips and busy tongue, urging excited juices from the well of her cunt, a veritable stream coursing over my jaw as I kissed and tickled her nether mouth and our sordid surroundings dissolved around us, her moans answered by my own as the surly waitress lifted my unempty bottle and started to walk away with it so that I had to go after her, and came back to find my seat taken by some barrel-built slob with three days' growth on his face, three weeks' grease on his skin, three months' dirt on his clothes, three years' filth on his mind, and three decades' heavy-labour strength in his muscles, all of which decided me to leave his theft unchallenged, although I did say, I believe, "Uh—excuse me, but that's my seat," to which he replied by looking puzzledly down to what small portion of the chair could be considered, through generous interpretation, as visible beneath his hanging gut, and then with a grotesque contortion of his unwieldy bulk, by peering curiously at what his obstructed vision I suppose construed as the back of the chair and, finally, by declaring, in a voice whose quality was reminiscent of a maltreated cement mixer, and whose tone strove to approach what somewhere in the scarred reaches of his damaged brain he doubtless hoped could be considered an air of ingenuousness, "I dohn' see no *name* on it," a witticism to which I responded with ominous glare—or so I thought, till I caught in the mirror behind him an image of a cowed visage with a look in its eyes of mingled terror and hurt disappointment, tempered nonetheless with a kind of steely pride (even in the worst of situations, I do have, however much most people I know might doubt it, some shred of dignity), the upshot of which was that I retreated with a glower (or was it an air of deference?) to a less favourably situated point, a bench seat to the right and rear of my oversized usurper, there to sip desultorily at my warming beer while calculating the largest areas of the stage I could make accessible to my vision by what possible points I could arrange to have my head at, allowing for such factors as patrons present and imminent, stalled waitresses, itinerant drinkers, perambulating whores, and whatever other obstructions the business of the establishment and the whims of its occupants might throw up between me and the magnet that drew me to this inhospitable environment, where I'd undergone an hour of waiting in the front-row centre chair and a half-hour of fidgeting on the bench beneath the mirror facing the stage she finally took, to the accompaniment of sultry rock music and scattered applause, strutting and smiling and spinning so that the tiny skirt of her black lingerie tunic lifted saucily to reveal the stately grandeur of her buttocks, bisected by the black strand of her G-string. She continued in this vein throughout the length of one song, her eyes sparkling, her body flashing, her flesh asserting its nakedness beneath the scant outfit, from which peeked now a breast, now a buttock, now the graceful sweep of back, belly, thigh; her hands, with slim, tapering fingers, tracing delicate designs in the air or beckoning enticingly, stroking her inner thighs or pressing over her breasts and down her sides, accentuating the curves of her torso, until the one song ended and the next began, in a new and slower rhythm that she fitted her movements to without a second's pause, slowly removing, with taunting smile, the black belt of her tunic that hung now loosely about her and eventually slipped first from one shoulder, only to be lifted back, then from the other, lifted back, then let slip entirely, lifted back, and finally divested as the second song segued into the third and she stood swaying, undulating her hips, in only the black G-string, at the front centre of the stage, holding the black belt out in front of her with both hands, smiling and beckoning, causing the lummox in front of me to heave to his feet and lumber towards her, at which she shook her head and hands, taking a few rapid steps back, laughing, saying, "No-ho-ho-ho...not you," then pointing finger and eye directly at me and intoning "Him!"—at which the massive, shaggy, grimy head revolved slowly, like a cumbersome turret on an ungainly tank, to level a salvo of blistering glares on vindicated me, who stood and approached without a glance at his retreat, my eyes fixed on the smiling and near-naked beauty who looped the slender fabric of her belt around my neck, once and twice, creating a kind of leash with which she pulled the upper portion of my body towards her on the raised platform, inducing me to bend forward as she backed away and strutted along the platform's length, leading me to left, to right, to centre, where she stopped, holding my head at the level of her chest, shook her breasts in slow, quivering enticement before me, then turned and guided her rump into my line of vision, half-turned again, straightening up with my head at her haunch, which she bumped towards me and away, towards me and away, making and breaking contact with the wet kisses I lavished on the soft, voluptuous curve of flesh that finally ceased its rocking motion as my tongue found its way to the cool surface of her skin, upon its doing which she took a final retreat, thrust a red licorice whip in my mouth, unlooped her belt, turned me round, and launched me back to my seat with a gentle push amid the cheers and laughter of the crowd, from which she selected a second honoured member to whom she administered the same tantalizing treatment, the execution of which led me to realize that the licorice whip she had rewarded me with had been tucked in her G-string strap at her hip; that I was to have attempted to get hold of it with my teeth while she made of it, by her dancing motion, a moving target; that she had finally conceded my failure to recognize the point of the exercise and brought it to an end by manually presenting me with the prize I was to have orally acquired; which acquisition my successor in the little game brought off with an adroitness that won him cheers from the crowd, cheers that gave way to applause for Black Satin, who concluded her performance with a sensual strut round the stage, scooping up her robe and donning it as she descended the few steps to the floor and I arose to intercept her on her passage through the aisle in front of the platform, anticipating the warm smile reserved for so favoured a one as me, whose gallant invitation to buy her a drink produces an even warmer smile, a gentle squeeze of my arm, a breathy "Thank you—of course! First table in front of the bar, just as soon as I get into some clothes," and a sashay down the length of the club to the stairs descending to the dressing room, from which she soon emerges in a flouncy flowered summer dress, eyes bright, smile dazzling, talking with animated delight about all the many things we find so swiftly that we have in common, through one drink, two drinks, until finally: "Oh, hold my drink here for me till I finish my one last go onstage for the night," and I do and she does and she's back at the table and finishes her drink and leaves on my arm to take a turn or two with me through the rollicking late-night crowds on the brightly lit downtown streets before announcing her wish for some rocking and bopping at an after-hours underground booze can she knows, where we go and dance and party the night away, ending with me escorting her home ("Your place? Sure."), leaving a hoarse-voiced message on the office's overnight answering machine that I've come down with something and won't be in to work that day, and spending blissful hours making love with her, sleeping, waking, making love again, planning all the things we'll do together over the ensuing weeks, except that, just as I begin to stride towards her, having risen from my seat at the end of the dance, I feel the boot-clad right foot of the maleficent oaf who had earlier ousted me from my front-row seat precipitately interposed between my legs, bringing me to the floor in a sprawl, my eyes confronted by the proximate vision of two dainty toes, with red-painted nails, jutting from the tip of Black Satin's right shoe.

I clambered to my feet, regaining my composure, if not my dignity, amid the boorish choked cackles of my tormentor and his companions. Black Satin looked at me somewhat askance, and with a small "Excuse me" stepped round me and proceeded on her way. Abashed but undaunted, I decided to press what little advantage I had—no advantage at all, really, except that she was there, within speaking distance. Concealing as best I could, with contrived casual outward demeanour, my inner sense of desperation that no other such opportunity might present itself to fulfill the destiny I felt was ours, I hastened after her and asked in a tone that I hoped communicated an air of diffidence, assertiveness, respect, and aplomb, if she would be kind enough to grace me with her presence at a table down near the door for a drink and a brief conversation. Clearly, my refined phrasing of the request pierced through whatever veil of mistrust she might wrap herself in against the unwelcome advances of strangers in such unsavoury surroundings, for she replied without hesitation, "Sure. Singapore Sling. But give me ten minutes to put on my nail polish," doubtless perceiving that here was no basely motivated hustle, no common pass, but rather an earnest approach from a man of honest sensitivity—nobility, even—whose interest was sparked by a perception of her finer attributes as a person, not merely her manifest physical charms. Ten minutes? Hah! Twenty, thirty, forty-five, an hour!—they would seem as nothing, once rewarded by the privilege of her company for as much as five minutes, even if a Singapore Sling should prove to be the most expensive cocktail the establishment were to offer. Which indeed was the case. As was the twenty, thirty, forty-five minutes, an hour; at the end of which time she finally appeared, in jeans and T-shirt, from the staircase leading to the washrooms below and, ignoring me and the now tepid, watery Singapore Sling, hooked her arm, with effusive and enthusiastic greeting, into that of some slim, tight-buttocked young stud at the bar, who welcomed her with a warmly returned open-mouthed kiss and a salacious grab at her denim-clad ass before abandoning his barely touched drink to swirl out the door with her into the sweltering night—no, it was spring and cool...or, no, fall and nippy...they both had on windbreakers...no, wait...fur coats, winter. At any rate, they left, caught up immediately in the tawdry parade of downtown revellers who...actually, the streets were deserted, well, perhaps sparsely populated...or, well, I don't really know...but anyway, they left and I was glad I hadn't given in to the impulse I'd felt, while waiting for her, to rush out into the street and chase a block or two down to where some street vendor was parked behind a pathetic little stand ranked with bunches of flowers—roses, chrysanthemums, marigolds—to throw down a couple of dollars and grab the cellophane-wrapped bouquet and dash back to the Barbados, ignoring the importunate whores outside the grubby dive—sad, unbecoming women, caked with makeup, decked out in cheap, tight-fitting dresses that were supposed to fire off, in the hungry male mind, fantasies of wanton lust, forbidden pleasure amid silken opulence, easy virtue surrendered willingly in a mist of soft fabric and softer flesh: pitiful girls, of no real sexuality, asking incongruously, "Want a date, mister?" as though they'd never had a date in their lives and the surreptitious fuck in some seedy walk-up crib, or the quick blow job in a car down a dark lane, would make up for that, and the few bucks they earned would compensate them for the beatings they endured from dissatisfied pimps who thought they should have made more: "Fuckin' bitch! Y're holdin' back on me, ain'tcha? Ain'tcha?!" and back on the street with more bruises, now even less appealing and still less capable of making the expected amount, and on and on until they wind up god knows where, scrounging in some slum or wandering the streets with all their earthly possessions in shopping bags...past that and back into the tinselly, raucous, good-timing, colour-lit atmosphere of the Barbados, where a guy leans over to me at my table to ask, "Want a woman?" and I say, "No."

And No, I think to myself. No, I think. No, I don't want "a" woman, I want "the" woman, I want *her*, I want Black Satin, whatever her real name is, I want *her*, I want the elegant, intelligent, witty, warm, beautiful, sensitive, giving human being I imagine and believe her to be.

Glad I didn't do that. Glad I didn't rush down the street and waste my money on unwanted flowers, unappreciated gifts. Glad I only lost one hour out of a lifetime of valuable hours, till she walked away with someone else.

I hung around for five minutes or so. Finished my beer. Left, leaving the cheap little cellophane-wrapped bouquet on the table behind me.

4

I don't know why I dream these images. The woman resembles—but is not—my mother, who could never conceive of donning such apparel. The leather doesn't befit her aged flesh, nor the studs her conventional morals, which would be further outraged by the skimpiness of the black attire in which she appears before me, whip in hand, seductive expression suffusing her features as she lures and entices me, urging me close to her wrinkled loins, her sagging breasts, her pale skin and bulging veins. The dream recurs. Each time there is a slight acceleration of my arousal. Her gray hair sweeps across my face as she leans over me, a wanton smile playing across her features, the smile mixed with an expression of some little bemusement, of, perhaps, a kind of concern, as though she knows that this is what's required of her, though she is not sure why, or perhaps is not really sure that it *is* what's required of her, but persists in it anyway, flaunting herself, tempting me with promises of pleasures undreamt of, leading me on, raising my hopes and my penis, bringing my passion to such a peak of intensity that nothing else exists, not just for me, but absolutely—nothing, nothing else but this intense self-nurturing bond of desire, fired by the great folds of her ample flesh, the vast sag of her belly, the multiple bulges of wan flab, pinched into so many bulbs by the tight costume and tighter laces that crisscross her bosom, her thighs, her sack-like arms, her massive calves becoming lumpy ankles that blend into her bloated feet, whose toes are so many swollen slugs I find my mouth descending to in slavering desire, sucking and licking, oblivious to the coarse texture of the slipper straps that squeeze against the straining flesh. She is, of course, not my mother, so unlike the fragile, thin-limbed, frail-built woman who bore me, bred me, succoured and seduced me—no, I mean *re*duced me, that is, I mean *in*duced me, I mean *excused* me: excused my faults, my inabilities, my failures, my feebleness, my sinful, evil attitudes that caused her so much pain, seeing me err in matters moral, social, physical, emotional, spiritual, and nutritional, inflicting on her, as I did, the agony of expectation, the unfulfilled promise of brilliance, the teasing display of talents unrealized, gifts ignored, intellect undisciplined, the continuing disappointments of finances disorganized, hair unkempt, body unwashed, clothes in disarray, studies neglected, nails untrimmed, beard ungroomed, career abandoned, sexuality stunted, chances missed, opportunities unpursued, correspondence unanswered, bills unpaid, words misspelled, grammar inaccurate, manners forgotten, milk spilt, bed wet, food dribbled, pants shit; I was a recalcitrant infant, child, son, person, being—beneath contempt and beyond hope. And she, whoever she is, this woman in my dream (not my mother, oh certainly not my mother, who was not fat, not frail, not somewhere in between, not kind, not cruel, not beautiful, ugly, short, tall, nor glamorous, nor plain, nor stingy, nor generous, but simply my mother), this woman, whose image arises continually before me amid the sluggish vapours of my sleeping mind, is nothing like my mother, whose plump paws I remember paddling incessantly on my vulnerable buttocks in retribution for deeds the repercussions of which were clearly so vast (though incomprehensible to me) as to deserve the unrelenting assault on my hindmost parts that the slender, tapering fingers of her delicately formed hands administered so punitively to my welcoming flesh, grateful for the physical absolution granted it, flesh undeserving of the forgiveness thus mercifully awarded, bearing with it relief so sweet that I would soon, with instinct blind but unerring, perpetrate some new enormity to earn yet another rain of grace upon the dry plain of my implacable rump that shrank (as my soul in terror shrank) from each fresh blow the heartless bitch let fall in the painful cascade of smacks and wallops she poured so relentlessly, so regularly upon me.

The dream recurs. Each time there is a slight variation in her. Each time her gray hair sweeps across my wrinkled loins, my pale skin and bulging veins, my bloated body, so ill-befitting the skimpy black attire in which I appear before her. I don't know why I dream. These images recur: the whip in hand, the seductive expression, the woman who is strange to me, the thin-limbed, frail-built, fragile being whose sack-like arms and massive calves nurture a kind of concern, an expression of bewilderment, as though I know that this is what's required of me but am not sure why, or perhaps am not really sure that it *is* what's required of me, but persist in it anyway, succoured and seduced each time the whip recurs, descending on my vulnerable buttocks, tempting me with promises of pleasures undreamt of, my sagging breasts, my lumpy ankles that blend into bloated feet whose toes are so many swollen slugs I find my mouth descending to in slavering desire, sucking and licking, bed wet, food dribbled, diapers shit, a rain of grace upon my parched soul that shrinks in terror from the recurring dream, the gray hair that sweeps across me, the conventional morals, the wanton smile playing across the features of the woman I don't know. Why, I dream these images. I don't. I know I don't. I dream other images. I dream the beautiful woman who approaches me with a soft smile and touches me knowingly, tenderly, expertly, just back of my balls and forwards along, thrilling soft sensations the lengths of the nerves there, giving promise of pleasures soon to be realized, soon to be gray, soon to be sagging, soon to be flesh. The dream recurs.

5

From my vantage point in the second balcony at the symphony concert, as the orchestra tuned and pre-concert chatter filled the hall, I surveyed the audience below and felt a small flower of...what?—fear, anxiety, excitement, a composite of all of these?—blossom in my stomach, radiating up to my heart and chest and down through my guts to my balls, where the flower's petals set up a tickling and tingling, stirring my dormant member to a kind of preliminary roll, a torporous list to left or right, as my eyes fell on a figure seated in the centre of the twentieth row or so—a figure tiny at this distance, a figure of whom I had a three-quarters front view (my seat being on the side balcony), a figure whose features I could not quite make out, a figure my companion at the symphony (a cosmetics company marketing woman with cultural pretensions and marital yearnings) was oblivious to, a figure I knew to be that of Black Satin, knew by the soft sheen of her hair, the smoothness of her pale complexion, the erotic ruby gloss of her lipstick, the elegant lift of her chin, the sophisticated carriage that would be evident were she standing instead of sitting, the quivering of her breasts within her low-cut evening gown as she laughs warmly in appreciation of some joke or bon mot that has just been communicated to her, gracefully crossing her slender legs with a whisper of black stocking on black stocking, the slit at the side of her dress disclosing, as a result of this movement, a white sliver of thigh at the top of the stocking on her right leg, suggesting that she is wearing a garter belt, doubtless a black one (since her dress and stockings are black), its straps surely trimmed with strips of delicate black lace stretching from the belt itself, at her waist, over the luxurious curves of her buttocks, across a minuscule wisp of fabric clinging to the moist warmth of her vulva as she sat there some eighty or a hundred feet beneath me and I cursed myself for not bringing binoculars and tried to discern whether that last glance upwards was in my direction and whether it fell on me and she recognized me and there flashed briefly across her features a slight start of surprise or excitement or pleasure at being with me at the symphony, resting her head with casual affection on my shoulder, absently stroking my thigh as we're bathed in the lush orchestral sounds of a Tchaikovsky overture, every nuance of which can be discerned with absolute clarity in the seats I have chosen with such painstaking attention to the hall's acoustic properties and with no regard for cost, not wanting to stint on this special night out when we've both been able to squeeze some time from the demands of our respective careers (hers the new one of film producer), and she dips her head a bit to smell the rose I picked up from the florist on my way home and which she holds now amid the packed throng of the concert hall, a small smile of contentment playing over her lips as she drinks in the sensuous richness of the rose's fragrance and the spiritually refreshing sounds of the music, unaware that on a side balcony of the hall, high above her, so small in her vision that she could not make out a single detail of his features, a man sits in reluctant company with a cosmetics marketing woman, wishing he was instead with her, certain that she is now holding the rose he placed in her hand the night before, as she lay naked on the stage at the end of her dance, and plotting how he can manage to encounter her in the lobby during intermission, at a point when somehow both his companion and hers are elsewhere, to engage her in conversation about the concert and find a way to introduce himself and secure a future meeting, hoping she will not connect him with those other surroundings whose part in her life she surely wishes to play down, surroundings from which she will soon disengage herself to settle into a more savoury career—perhaps as a film producer—thereafter to share with him romantic evenings at symphony concerts, dressed in a black strapless dress, discreetly low-cut, her head lolling on his shoulder as her nostrils fill with the sweet, heady odour of a rose he has presented her with and, in his lap, the fingers of her left hand intertwining with the fingers of his right in abstracted, unguarded affection, even as they do now, while I watch from my high perch, peering to confirm that it is her, knowing beyond a shadow of a doubt that it is her, certain that it is her, thinking it is her, believing it is her, hoping it is her, wondering if it is, considering that it may not be, knowing.

◆　◆　◆

Boston or romaine, I wondered. Boston or romaine or both...standing in doubt by the fresh-produce counter in the supermarket, overwhelmed—as I usually am—by the profusion of vegetables to choose among: varieties of lettuce, broccoli, parsnips, cauliflower, turnips, rutabagas, radishes, carrots, zucchini, celery, a confusing welter of leaves and roots and seed casings, all of which complement, better or worse, an equally confusing range of meats and fishes and fowl, the mix of which I usually get wrong, finding myself each week standing before them in a state of fresh indecision, running through computations and recollections of which taste combinations pleased my palate over the last seven days, holding two small onions while musing distractedly, trying to recall whether I have a surplus or dearth of them at home, staring absently at a tangle of bean sprouts and wondering how many days they would survive should I lose my appetite for them between now and the time I prepare my dinner for today or tomorrow or the next day, settling in my mind whether the cucumber at home has reached a point of decay sufficient to warrant its replacement with another or, indeed, whether I enjoy cucumbers enough to warrant my ever purchasing them again at all—these deliberations or ones like them coursing through my brain this one particular day when I stood debating, oh, not the relative merits of Boston or romaine or both, but the advisability of steaming string beans or sautéeing snow peas with my fillet of haddock, or perhaps whether or not I would want to include mushrooms in the salad I might assemble mid-week (it being summer and I being partial to salads mid-week in the summer) (unless it was winter and I was considering the most prudent quantity of potatoes to purchase for mashing and covering in hot gravy, to accompany the roast I'd bought to comfort and warm me against the chills of the season), when I saw her there, summer or winter, fall or spring, her, there, amid the tiered rows of produce—vegetables and fruit—there in her rich furs or shorts and halter top or light coat or jeans and windbreaker, looking not like a goddess with power to make me cringe and beg for a favoured glance or stand proud and erect when granted some small, unsolicited attention, not a Black Satin doll of imperial bearing and forbidding presence, but a woman buying vegetables, a girl who looked no more certain than I about the prudence of having chicken share a plate with fried onions or an omelette with a baked potato, a lady, moreover, who had a little garland of tiny pimples sprouting on her left temple, covered up some with a coating of makeup, but visible nonetheless—a person, simply: human and vulnerable and present and approachable. Certainly approachable. Men approach women in situations like this every day. I have done so myself on innumerable occasions. There's nothing to it. Simply glance across the counter spread with apples or oranges (it was such a counter, set in the middle of the aisle, that she stood at, on the other side from me) and say, "Are these good for baking?" (if apples) or "Would these be the best for juicing, do you think?" (if oranges) and away you go, launched on a little pond of conversation that, with remarks on the weather, can grow to a small lake, and from there expand through a wealth of topics to a sea, an ocean, the two of you sailing happily about on it until it's the most natural thing in the world to say, "You like Bartók? But they're playing his second piano concerto just next week at the symphony! Why, I believe—yes, I do…I have a pair of tickets" (you don't, but that can be attended to that afternoon at the symphony box office—a mere trifle) "I'd be delighted to have you join me…if you'd like," and there you are, a week later, sitting in the symphony, her with a rose you bought for her, leaning her head on your shoulder with a dreamy smile on her lips. So I asked, "Would these be the best for juicing, do you think?" (my heart in my throat) and she looked over, rather casually, and replied, "I don't know anything about juicing onions" (I was holding a large red onion), at which, of course, I laughed and said, "No, I meant the oranges," to which she replied with a blank look, a hint of suspicion around her eyes, and the flat remark "These are apples." I was wondering how to get from there to Bartók, when she eyed me now with open suspicion and began to move pointedly off towards the frozen food department.

The shopping cart I'd picked up on entering the store had a reluctant right front wheel and a left rear one in need of oil, so that my progress was accompanied by an annoying little duet of scrapes and squeaks, not that I paid it any heed, my peregrinations through the aisles being undertaken in a state of preoccupation, looking less at the rows and stacks of canned and packaged foods than at the ends of the aisles where I might catch a glimpse of Black Satin—which I did, once or twice, each time a thrill coursing through me, a weakening of the knees, a drop of the stomach, as though her presence before me created an absence within me—my course through the store being dictated not so much by my gastronomic needs as by my calculation of when she would arrive at the checkout counter, so that I could be there immediately or soon after, following her out at a discreet distance, but near enough to notice her consternation at her car door, where she stood, grocery bags on the ground, searching through her purse, trying all the pockets of her coat and jeans (if it was winter or fall or spring), and finally peering through the window, doubtless at the sight of her keys dangling from the ignition, at which point I appear beside her to announce that I'll get a wire coat hanger from the store and have her inside her car in seconds, though of course it's more like minutes, during which I eradicate any bad impression that may have been created by my awkwardness at the fresh-produce counter—not by any direct allusion to that unfortunate scene but by simple force of presence and proficiency in the task at hand and purity of motive: to help someone out of a jam, which she obviously appreciates, talking warmly of this and that, revealing an interest in music, Bartók especially, at which point I go to mention that his second piano concerto is on at the symphony the following week, but suddenly recall that I have no idea of the symphony program for next or any other week and instead mumble something about having a fair collection of recordings of Bartók works—concerti and other orchestral pieces—and then realize that this may sound like some sleazy pre-proposition and so fall rather silent, leery of making a bad impression, and besides I need to concentrate pretty hard on where the tip of the wire is going inside her car, which is a late-model import with no knobs on the push locks, which means I have to hook the handle to get it open, which I finally do, and she's inside in a trice, thanking me and saying, "Maybe we'll bump into each other at a concert someday," and I approach the checkout counter, making my way through and paying and walking out the door wondering why there's no sign of her and then realizing that the cashier is calling me back to pick up my purchases, which I'd left behind and which I retrieve and carry to my car, finding my keys locked inside and seeing Black Satin pull away in a late-model import.

◆　◆　◆

Music pounded, guests chattered, dancers writhed, and multi-hued lights beamed down, up, and across, bathing the bacchanal in a variegated glow that made ambiguous the movements, attire, physiques, and features of the heaving mass of revellers who had responded to the invitation to "Come and be UNZIPPED—the party of the decade in the decade of the party! Get out of the office, out of the studio, out of the closet, out of the rat race, and out of your *mind* at UNZIPPED. *Come* to it and *be* it!" and who now overflowed a warehouse loft hung with streamers, bedecked with zipper-imprinted banners, layered with smoke, and charged with the kind of chaotic energy that the mix of crowds, music, drink, and drugs engenders.

Having exhausted what little conversational possibilities there were with the few friends and acquaintances I had so far encountered among the throng, I was wandering aimlessly, looking half-heartedly for the gorgeous dark-haired woman who had earlier talked with me in enthusiastic tone for half an hour, danced with me lethargically for two numbers, and then suddenly excused herself to, she said, go and talk with her sister over there. I found myself at the edge of the gyrating mass of dancers and was approached by a young blond-haired man who struck up a conversation with me about theatre, mainly delivering, with a slight smirk, cynically dismissive observations on any and every recent local production and prominent personality. About the point at which he'd begun resting his hand lightly on my chest as he spoke to me, and moving his knee against mine for the third or fourth time, despite my having moved away a bit at each contact, I noticed the dark-haired beauty amid a sea of spinning, stomping bodies, dancing in a close and steamy, hip-grinding embrace with her "sister," who, from the looks of her, was probably a fashion model. "Excuse me," I said to the young cynic (interrupting his denunciation of some current production because "the wardrobe is just tacky"), "but I think I see my mother over at the bar," where what I did see, and soon joined, was a congestion of shoving patrons calling out orders to barkeeps who couldn't hear them or were busy getting orders they *had* heard. I finally managed to get a drink and, turning from the bar to make my way through the jam that confronted me, jostled someone's arm, eliciting a cry of "Shit!" and simultaneously experiencing the sensation of something cold and wet in the area of my crotch. Uttering a spontaneous apology, I found myself facing a look of controlled annoyance—lips pursed and pulled down at one corner, eyes glaring—on the face of Black Satin, who stood before me in a short white dress with frills at bodice and hem, her hand dripping with some of the same liquid that was soaking my slacks, her look of annoyance not softened by my offer to replace her drink, an enterprise we both knew to hold little promise of swift conclusion, especially since we'd already been moved back a rank or two by an influx of obstreperous customers, and so I did the only thing *to* do under the circumstances, which was to offer her *my* drink, earning myself a look escalated from annoyance to exasperation—eyes cast briefly ceilingwards, head tilted slightly back, mouth open in silent sigh—at which I asked, "What *can* I do?" and her face relaxed and she shrugged and smiled and said, "Dance?" and so I did a little soft-shoe and looked at her with my most beguiling is-that-okay smile and her smile broadened and she gave a little giggle and I said, "I think I saw an inch or two of space over by the pillar on the left," and we were on the dance floor, wriggling and writhing and laughing, and after a couple of numbers she said she had to disappear for a bit but she'd see me later and I could replace that drink for her, and I told her my name and asked her hers and she replied, "Blackie," and was gone.

After about half an hour, with my pants now relatively dry and another hard-won drink in hand, I was lingering in a sparsely populated area by a small, chest-high platform divided into two circular sections and set at the end of the room opposite the dance floor, both sections of the platform backed by curtains—one black, one white—each curtain bisected by a large zipper. At the other end of the room, on the mainstage, the band ended a tune, and someone of indeterminate gender, clad in a pink jacket with broad padded shoulders, a sequined gray shirt and elaborately draped white pants, leapt onto the stage, grabbed a mike and screamed—in a voice whose pitch failed to resolve the enigma of its originator's sex—"ARE YOU GETTING UNZIPPED?!" to which a roar of "YES!" arose as from one throat, eliciting a squeal of delight from the question mark onstage, who screamed even louder, "ARE YOU UNZIPPED *ENOUGH*?!"—the antiphon to which was a lusty "NOOOO!" with some scattered contrapuntal

"YEAH!"'s. "Well," (voice lowered in volume, with a seductive, wait'll-you-hear-this tone entering in) "ladies and gentlemen and ambiguities," (laughter) "have we got something for *you*. You are about to witness" (voice beginning a continuing crescendo) "a Young Lady Who Is Going to Get More UNZIPPED THAN YOU COULD EVER *HOPE* FOR! BACK *THERE*," (a spotlight brightened the stage I stood by) "DANCING FOR YOUR DELIGHT—THE ONE...THE ONLY...*BLACK SATIN!*" and the drummer seemed to hit every drum he had all at the same time, as the guitar wailed and the bass pounded, lights swirled and the white curtain parted with the descent of its giant zipper to reveal Black Satin, clad in a black-leather jumpsuit seamed and lined with broad steel zippers, posing with fist on jutting hip, her head tossed haughtily back, arrogant eye surveying the crowd that surged from dance floor and bar to this new focus of interest, pressing me up against the platform as Black Satin strode to the centre of the stage and snapped into a jerky, contortive sequence of virtuosic steps and moves that caused the leather to strain enticingly against back and shoulder and breast and belly, thigh and hip and buttock and crotch, until she took a leap and landed in the splits, her left arm bent at the elbow, held beneath her breasts to lift them slightly, her right hand raised to her parted lips, forefinger held to her upper front teeth, her landing perfectly timed to another explosion from the drums, followed by a brief silence, during which a salacious smile spread over her face and the band took up a sensual bump-and-grind rhythm and a woman, pressed against my back by the crush of spectators, her mouth by my ear as she craned her neck to see past me, breathed, "Oooohhhh, she's going to undo all those zippers..." and I couldn't tell if the excruciating thrill that swept down my spine and fluttered through my genitals was brought on by the tickle of her breath at my ear, the arousal that her voice betrayed, or the anticipation of the process (the eventuality of which there was none more aware than I) that she announced—and which began to transpire, as Black Satin drew herself up and strutted provocatively around the stage, toying first with a zipper at the top of her left leg, then with one that crossed her right breast, now one running down her left arm, now another at the back of her neck, until someone started chanting, "Un-zip! Un-zip! Un-zip!" and the crowd took it up, Black Satin glorying in the power she wielded, smiling and teasing, as the emcee howled over the music, "STILL MORE TO BE UNZIPPED! FOR THOSE OF YOU WITH DIFFERENT TASTES...RAM-ROD!" at which the black curtain parted in the wake of another descending zipper and there appeared a muscular young man in a white leather peaked cap, an abbreviated white leather jacket, a pair of tight white leather pants with a pronounced bulge at the crotch, white ankle-top boots, a profusion of black metal zippers studding jacket and pants, his arrival producing a chorus of piercing shrieks, one of which sends an arrow of pain through my right eardrum, as Ramrod whirls and spins and squeezes his tight buttocks inside his tight pants and smiles under his trim moustache and leers at a woman in the crowd, then flexes his pectorals, arms bent and held shoulder-high, fists in, elbows out, biceps straining against the white leather sleeves, jacket riding up from his flat, hair-matted belly, pelvis rocking languorously, while on my left I see, out of the corner of my eye, the cynical young blond who held a low opinion of the plays in town and a high opinion of me, his gaze fixed on Ramrod, who's back in motion, not so much dancing as executing a sequence of acrobatic postures that fit in time with the music to which Black Satin is undulating, her left hand on her left hip, fingers playing with the zipper clasp there, a pout on her lips as she directs a look of impish seduction at someone in the crowd, then dips slowly to the left, drawing the zipper down, creating a slit that shows first a slash of hip, then an expanse of thigh with a hint of rounded buttock at the top, then her knee, calf, ankle, the leather falling away from the slender length of her leg and the voice in my right ear saying, "Mmmmm, sex-y! Now let's see the hunk unzip..." which the hunk obligingly does, peeling a zipper down the inside of his right pant leg as women squeal and he grins and lowers himself on one knee, left leg outstretched, eyeing a lady in the crowd, raising his eyebrows inquiringly, pointing to the zipper clasp on his other pant leg, beckoning with a finger till someone lifts the girl up so she can reach across the stage to pull down the zipper for him, managing, in the course of things, to brush her hand across that spectacular bulge, then working the zipper down very slowly, trailing her forefinger along the inside of his leg and smiling at him as he smiles back and slowly shakes the finger he beckoned her with, in mock admonishment now, as the crowd begins to clap rhythmically and sway from side to side, carrying me with it and causing me, pressed against the stage as I was, to acquire an incidental further stimulation where no further stimulation was required, the condition heightened still more by the crowd's motion creating a maddening friction against my back from the voluptuous body of the woman behind me, so that I endeavoured to assuage matters some by pressing my buttocks back to withdraw my pelvic area from the front of the platform, which action, I guess, was misinterpreted by the lady behind, who ground her groin against me, thereby renewing contact between me and the front of the stage, atop which Black Satin pranced, undoing the zippers that held her leather leggings on, their removal reducing her jumpsuit to a remnant cut high over her hips, tapering down over her buttocks to strap-width at the crotch, a zipper dissecting the entire torso section of the jumpsuit, from the nape, down the back, under, around, and up to the front of her neck, her lovely neck, her graceful neck, which she stretches, leaning her head back to let her hair fall free and nearly touch the lush bulge of her buttocks, hugged by the tiny leather *v* that allows so ample a view of them, my eyes rivetted there as she tips forward, bending down, advancing her taut ass towards the point where I stand, swaying and sweating and pressed against from behind and, now, from the side, where the blond cynic—inspired, I guess, by the sight of Ramrod—has managed to turn a bit towards me and make apparent, by an unmistakable stiffness that presses against my thigh, his pleasure in the whole enterprise, which progresses with rapidly proliferating ripping of zippers and flaunting of flesh: Black Satin doing the splits in front of me, her trim derriere straining against the leather, inches from my face, Ramrod rubbing his hands over the hair on the inside of his thighs, the muscles there tensed hard, sculpted, as are all the muscles in his well-shaped legs, the crowd crying, "Un-zip! Un-zip!" her breasts spilling out before my enraptured eyes, his jacket pulled back from out-thrust chest as he struts round the platform whose fringe bristles with a

forest of straining female arms towards which he advances and
withdraws, prompting shrieks and imprecations and shrill
laughter, his fingers playing with the wiry sandy hair that curls
over his chest, the lush swell of her buttocks revealed by the
parting of the leather, nothing on now but his bulging leather
pouch and ankle-top boots, the latter of which he smilingly
offers for removal by the clamouring horde, willing hands
responding, the woman behind saying, "Niiiiice feet!" which I
silently, fervidly agree with, fixing my gaze on the lithe and
delicate right foot of Black Satin, where a slight black slipper
conceals only the sole and part of the toes, and I trail my eyes
along the slim length of her leg to the folds of her vulva,
which is now stretched open before me, the zipper progressing along the gentle rise of her belly, the white pouch, secured
on either side by short tracks of zipper, thrust towards the
spectators, grinding first to left, then to right, breasts squeezed
together by elbows, left hip flirting with the hand that's
extended the furthest and that finally reaches one last inch and
rips the zipper down to expose a tuft of pubic hair, the tawny,
vulnerable flesh near the genitals, a pang of arousal surging
through me as nipples are pinched and buttocks caressed, right
hip now bumping towards and away from the rippling sea of
arms on the other side of the stage, a metal-trimmed garment
of black leather sliding down a leg, and a hand makes contact
with the zipper and yanks, the white leather pouch falling to
the stage and "Oooooohhh, he's got a hard-on..." sighed at my
ear in awed tones, as I pull away from the physically importunate blond cynic, who importunes further, and from the
woman behind, who grinds more against me, a smile from the
stage, upside-down between parted legs, deep knee bends,

cock bobbing enticingly, breasts kneaded and nipples pulled, P.A. blaring a screeching voice that asks, "IS THERE NO END?!" answers itself with "WELL, THERE'S SURE MORE!" and ends by announcing, "FOR YOUR FUR-THER DELECTATION—*JACK HAMMER!*" and I'm onstage in a hard hat, a red neckerchief, an open denim vest, rolled-bottom denim shorts, and leather gloves, a smile on my face for the screaming mass that crowds the platform on which I posture and pose, then hold my fists before me at hip-level and simulate the kind of body-shaking vibrations caused by operating a jackhammer, a visual double entendre that meets with a din of whistling, shouting appreciation, and I stop abruptly and begin to grind my hips, pull back my shoulders to show off my chest, run my hands down the flat, muscular trimness of my stomach, and stride the perimeter of the stage, then move to the centre to peel off my vest and kick off my boots and spin and dance and play with the zipper at the front of my shorts, tantalizing the woman behind me who is there before me, laughing and reaching and shouting, Black Satin beside her, white dress trimmed with frills at bodice and hem, swirling a drink that she rests on the edge of the stage as she eyes me appraisingly, watching as I let the woman behind me before me pull down my zipper and pull off my shorts to a chorus of ohs and ahs, nothing on now but a blue silk jock-strap, a hard hat and neckerchief, feeling a bit of a breeze on my butt from the waving arms as I parade round the stage, pose, dance, tease, and entice, drop down and do push-ups, tensing every muscle in my body, a grin on my face, feeling the eyes upon me as hands caressing my flesh, erect in my tiny blue jock, stomach churning with erotic urgency, laughing and teasing, a chant of "Lum-ber! Lum-ber!" building in soprano crescendo, till I comply, and the rolling chant erupts into a din of laughter and shrieks of delight, my eye falling, in the deafening pandemonium, on Black Satin, who leans an elbow on the stage and beckons slowly with one finger, luring me to the edge of the stage, where she's mouthing a word that I can't make out till I put my ear to her lips and she shouts, "Swizzlestick!" her hand on my cock and her drink raised and my prick immersed in a cold shock, bits of ice bumping against the swollen head, then an enveloping warmth and a tickle of tongue as she licks her swizzlestick and smiles down at me from the stage I stand before, gazing rapturously up at her in her pose of mock modesty: one leg bent inwards, her hand over her mound, an arm across her breasts, her mouth an *o* of pretended surprise, dozens of women now holding their drinks forth, calling, "Swizzle! Swizzle!" Ramrod doing a naked breakdance routine, the woman behind me rubbing her body unambiguously against me, the *o* of Black Satin's vulva displayed before me, my head between her legs, her head between mine, my hard hat hung on my cock, the woman behind me swirling her tongue in my ear, blowing hot rapid gusts of passion, a hand on my chin pulling my head to the side, a mouth locking on mine, tongue plunging deep, the kiss broken and the face of the cynical blond young man before me, his look tender and his voice soft, muttering, "Not tacky in the least," a curtain parting with the descent of a giant zipper, Black Satin emerging from a billowing cloud of dry-ice steam, clad in a black leather jumpsuit seamed and lined with broad metal zippers, coming in hard and loud on the downbeat, belting out a rock tune as Ramrod materializes beside her in white leather jacket and pants studded with a profusion of black zippers and adds harmony on the refrain, a large woman pulling at my neckerchief and shouting, "Take it off! Take it *all* off!" Black Satin running her hands feverishly through my hair, kissing my eyes, my cheeks, my lips, pressing my head downwards towards Ramrod's tumescent member that's jerking in tiny anticipatory spasms, the frenetic voice of the announcer screaming, "HAD ENOUGH?!" the band packing up, the crowd dispersed, someone in a hard hat pulling down zippers that flutter from the ceiling, me standing by the bar, pretty drunk, talking to one of the bartenders, who wears a denim vest and a red neckerchief, asking him if he remembers what the little dark-haired girl in the white dress with frills at bodice and hem was drinking and he repeats, incredulous, "Frills at bodice and hem?" over and over, "Frills at bodice and hem?" sweeping up broken glass, piling empty beer bottles into cardboard boxes, frowning and pulling his lips down in irritation, "Frills at bodice and hem?...Why don't you go home?"

◆ ◆ ◆

I don't remember whether I was on a legitimate client call that happened to be cancelled or was undergoing one of those days when the oppressive atmosphere of the office weighed my eyelids with the heaviness of lead, inducing me to inform my secretary that a visit to Nichol and Wah or Cochrane and Lee or some such client or other had proved necessary or advisable, thus finding escape from corporate confines and making my way through thin afternoon traffic to a downtown cinema, composing myself in a rear row for either a restful doze (should the film prove boring) or a relaxing watch, and having my composure shattered a few minutes later when I looked up and saw Black Satin seated at the end of the row of which I had been the previous sole occupant...at least, I was pretty sure the row had been empty—or perhaps I should say "am" pretty sure, for it is at the moment that I tell about it that I know for certain my belief about it and I'm not at all sure what I believed at the time that it happened...oh there's no question that it did happen: I have absolutely total recall of entering the cinema, purchasing a candy bar, drifting into the dimly lit auditorium, and selecting a row near the back; that much is certain, beyond dispute; it's the point at which Black Satin took a seat in the same row that remains in doubt, no such doubt at all about the fact that it was she who I saw there, dressed in the kind of baggy pants and layered tops that were in fashion then, no matter how impractical they might be, so that on a sultry summer day a woman like Black Satin would don a leotard-tight top, the kind which might reveal through its stretched fibres a hint of the flesh of her breasts or the suggestion of skin-tone on her sharply protuberant nipples, except that it has a sleeveless-vest sort of an affair looped over it, and maybe a loose, oversized shirt on top of that, so that the prospect of an air-conditioned theatre being hard to resist is not difficult to imagine, which is doubtless how she came to be at the same cinema as me, seated in the same row, a thin film of perspiration lining, in tiny beads, the upper lip of each of us, a small drop of sweat rolling, with shiver-producing chill, down our respective spines, a briny film of moisture between her breasts, a similar film broadened into a trickle between the cheeks of her ass, causing a dark stain to appear in the centre of the seat of her light cotton pants, within the confines of which her thighs were drying in the evaporative cool of the cinema—her thighs and, within the wispy, red, frilled silkiness of her panties, her genitals, silky themselves, but pink, not red, and private now, on a day off from working whatever club she was in that week or perhaps on an afternoon before going in to work the evening shift or maybe even relaxing during the interim between abandoning her one profession and taking up another, possibly that of film producer.

So, that much is known for sure: she was there. But had she entered and taken her seat before or after I arrived and sat down? I am pretty sure (or was, a few moments ago, when I first said "am"; I am less sure now, at this exact moment) that she was not there when I took my place, although whether I was at the time sure, I cannot say, memory being, after all, at best an imperfect medium for establishing reality, and mine at the time being less than it might be at its best, since her very presence—oh, of that I am sure: it was her, she *was* there…was (is, at any rate, here, in my recollection of the event) there in the fullness and perfection of her being, sweating, I guess, in the excessive clothing that fashion dictated (if it was, indeed, summer—and a hot day in that season—during which this all occurred) or perhaps warming up from the chill blasts of wind and snow that (were it winter, which it might have been) had buffeted her on her course to the theatre, so that she shucked her bulky down overcoat in the welcome heat of the auditorium, shaking melted snowdrops from her hair as she waited for the film to begin (and, incidentally, charming me by the grace with which she divested herself of her overcoat, and

arousing me by slouching down in her seat so that the loose
sweatshirt she wore hung loosely about her, accentuating the
swell of her bosom)...her very presence, as I was saying, created a dulling of my awareness to anything except her presence,
so that I was not—and am not yet—certain whether she took
her seat before I found my place in the centre of the row or
after, which is a matter of central importance: for if she was
there before I chose (oblivious to her presence) a row in
which she was already seated, it suggests that I was operating
on some kind of primeval radar that drew me (regardless of
such rationales as cancelled client calls or disaffections with
office environments) not only to the exact theatre she was to
attend but to the precise row in which she was to sit; and if
she instead arrived after I had taken my place and chose the
row in which I was seated, it suggests that she may have been
operating on a similar radar and, furthermore (since I know
that I was oblivious to her presence if she was there before I
chose that row to sit in, but have no way of knowing if she was
similarly oblivious to my presence there if she selected that
row after I was ensconced in one of its seats), that she may
have selected that row precisely because I was sitting in it, I
mean that she may have noticed me there, recognized me,
wanted to sit near me, but, being shy, contented herself with,
as it were, worshipping from afar, just as, say, at a symphony
concert, having spied me sitting some distance away, perhaps
in a second balcony when she is on the main floor, she might
maintain a diffident removal while entertaining the idea that
we were in fact attending the event together, even imagining
that the rose her escort had presented her with was in fact
given her by me, a small appreciation for the fine dinner I had

known she was preparing for me, a rose picked up at a florist's on the way home, a gesture I knew she would be pleased by, something for her to gratify her olfactory sense with while her auditory sense was bathed in the rich beauties of Dvorak's New World Symphony, enjoyed in the seats I had carefully selected with painstaking attention to the hall's acoustic properties, wanting to make this evening a special one, a small celebration of the second year of our being together, the relationship having been rocky but ultimately successful, though there were still disagreements about her making her living as a stripper, when I could provide her with as good a level of material comfort from the salary I earned as a middle manager.

So it wasn't surprising that, as the film progressed, the number of seats between us would diminish, not by any such crude measure as either of us rising and moving pointedly to the place beside the other, but by some ineluctable process that saw her leave and return with a bag of popcorn which she consumed, not in the seat at the end of the row, but in the one on the other side of her coat, two closer to me, which became four closer to me when I returned from a trip to the washroom and absent-mindedly entered the row from her end (a mildly surprised—certainly not annoyed—look on her face as she pulled in her legs to let me pass, not letting on that she recognized me, not even venturing a shy smile, which I would not have considered too forward: I, in fact, smiled at her—in an encouraging sort of a way—as I clambered past), repositioning myself two seats from my coat on the side towards her, which meant, in reality, not four but six seats fewer between us, which became eight fewer, I believe, when a late patron asked if the seat on which my coat lay was occupied and I

shook my head and took up my coat and put it on the seat I'd
been reclining in (I always put my feet up on the back of the
seat in front of me at the movies, and recline rather than sit in
the seat I occupy) and moved two seats over in the direction
of Black Satin, who was now about four or five seats away
from me, close enough, I felt, to warrant the occasional casual
remark about this or that scene in the movie, although I never
did feel enough at ease to actually say anything directly to her,
but instead laughed in a communicative sort of a way whenever something humorous transpired on the screen, doing
which, I once or twice glanced over, saw that she was laughing too, caught her eye, and felt as though we were sharing a
laugh, almost as though we were at the movies together,
which, of course, we were, in a way, but, of course, were not,
in another, more important way. Still, the movie was not yet
over and the possibility did remain that we might truly be
there together and be together too, in the future, at countless
other movies, perhaps, if things went the way I hoped, which
is why I'm sure I would have taken the opportunity presented by one of those times—I don't know, five or six, maybe,
possibly more—when our eyes met laughing over some silly
or touchingly humorous thing that happened in the
movie...taken the opportunity to make some little remark, a
telling insight, perhaps, about the main character or maybe
some witticism enlarging on the wit of the incident that
sparked our laughter—I know I would have done that, it
would have been just like me to do it and entirely unlike me
to miss or pass up such an opportunity, although I have no idea
now exactly what my remark was, but can attest that it was
clever enough to elicit a further little burst of laughter from

her, I think, unless (and this may be the case) it was that which made her turn her attention fixedly on the screen, casting the briefest sidelong glance in my direction a few seconds later, and thereafter avoiding any notice of my presence, which might have been intended as a rebuff (I don't remember if I considered that at the time, but I do now), although I expect it more likely that it was merely shyness on her part...I mean, you can't be too careful in a public place: you never know what kind of a dangerous person you might be encouraging, what kind of hurt or injury you may be letting yourself in for, so I was relieved by her aloofness, realizing that it indicated in her a healthy sense of self-preservation that would keep her from slipping heedlessly into some peril; it was not for her to know that she had nothing to fear from me, that my motives were the purest, my intentions the best: you just can't go around making exceptions to the general wise rule of conduct when a man you don't know is making advances...although she did know me, or at least had been invited for a drink by me and had talked briefly with me once in a corridor, had had her drink spilled by me and had danced with me, and really had no reason to think my intentions anything but the best, my approaches from the start having been respectful and deco-rous in the extreme, I myself a model of propriety, which (I now consider) may have been my big mistake, although damn it, if she hadn't been inured by all those years in tough dives like the ones she worked in, if she hadn't had the edges of her sensibilities and her innate good judgement of character dulled by daily contact with reprobates, users, con men, dope dealers, pimps, fences, thieves, mobsters, and the all-round no-good sons-of-bitches that were the regular inhabitants of her workplace, then she might have been a little more responsive, a little more receptive, a little more *realistic* about me, for chrissake, instead of acting like I had a knife down my pant leg or rape on my mind or Christ knows what kind of crazy stuff going around in her head that made her act like I was on another planet or something, treating me as though I had two heads or was some kind of freak or creep, so that I kept wanting to go up to her through this whole period and say, "Look, I'm not a drip. I'm not a pill. I'm no dumb cluck or nerd. I'm a relatively sensitive, reasonably decent—if, perhaps, excessively horny—human being, who wants to get to know you, certainly go to bed with you, possibly be in love with you, maybe grow old with you...all conditional on your willingness to proceed with each and every one of those stages, any of which would be, it is hoped, concluded without any hurt or harm, pain, grief, or disappointment to either of us, if such is possible in any human relationship of any depth or intensity" (which, of course—as I was to learn—it isn't), which speech I fortunately failed to gain the courage to address to her that day at the movies, for—as I saw on exiting into the bright glare of the early fall afternoon sun, turning back for one last look at her—she was not Black Satin but a girl of similar features, the differences not evident to me in the dim theatre light (I had strode through the lobby on my way out without managing to catch a front view of her), but all too apparent in the dusty glare on the street outside, where she made her way with downcast eye and swift and purposeful stride in the direction opposite to mine.

◆ ◆ ◆

There was a dinner party. No good reason to go, but no real reason not to. A slow social week for me, as I recall, so what the hell...My hosts' social circles barely overlapped with mine, so it was reasonable to anticipate the possible presence of some new and interesting people, which proved, during cocktails in the dining room, to be a vain hope. There was a female counterpart of the male jock there, a brash, abrasive, insecure sort of person whose approach to her self-perceived shortcomings was to adopt an air of bravado that resonated with all the richness and subtlety of a brass ball dropped into a shallow lead bowl; who recited as her own the latest popular opinions on everything from art to investment; and who laughed with a kind of grating bray. There was a sociology professor who kept talking about how the gathering at the party was a perfect cross-section of something or other, and who had the annoying nervous habit of whistling tunelessly and just barely audibly through his teeth whenever he was not speaking, the transition so effortless and apparently essential that it occurred even at pauses within single sentences or phrases that he uttered, so that his attempt, for example, to describe the physical location of a restaurant whose name he couldn't remember, might go something like "Well, (whistle, whistle) it's on the northeast corner of, uh, (whistle, whistle, whistle) oh what is the name of that street, I can never remember it, (whistle) well, anyway, the one with, you know, the sort of flat-iron building do they call it? on the west side and on the east, the (whistle, whistle, whistle, whistle) oh, I can't think of the name of it, but the insurance company there"—and on and on in that vein. There was a large smiling man with no opinion to offer on anything, who I suspected of speaking another language and lacking proficiency in English, until he made a public announcement of his need to use "the facilities" (as it pleased him to refer to the toilet). There was a man and a woman discovering a shared passion for the creation of verse and a shared disdain for the editors of literary journals throughout the country, who, they informed each other with mutually commiserative shock, had never accepted a single one of their poems, a state of affairs that they ultimately agreed was for the better, first of all, because they wouldn't want their work sharing the same pages with "the junk these rags publish," and second, because the publishing of one's poetry was, in fact (they wholeheartedly assured each other), a commercial activity, it being a much purer act to fashion it and retain it in the privacy of one's notebooks. I had retired into an accelerating taciturnity after sounding out a few of these folk on such topics as the home team's progress in its division (blank stares) and the best bands in the local bars (lowered eyebrows—as though someone had said "fuck" during tea at the rector's) and was entering into soulful communion with the cheeses and raw vegetables (which the female jock kept calling "crudités"), when there entered the room a tall, professorial-looking fellow with a rather benign, if somewhat absent, smile fixed on his face, and, pinned to his corduroy lapel, a largish metal button imprinted with the message "I Give Hugs." The male of the two poets with too much integrity to publish looked up, his expression subsiding from wrath at venal editors and hack bards to the kind of sappy, dewy-eyed smile that people with mixed feelings about babies sometimes lapse into when confronted with someone's latest offspring, and gave voice to the sentiment "Awwww, my kind of person...Can I have one?" which indeed he cloyingly could. The climate was getting so thick with marshmallow smiles that I feared suffocation, and therefore took off for the john, more as a defensive manoeuvre than as a response to any physical need, although I was, it's true, verging on surrender to the gag reflex.

The toilet tactic provided respite enough for me to consider my options, of which the only palatable one (peremptory departure) carried the near certainty of offending my hosts, with whom—much as I was beginning to doubt my interest in maintaining their friendship—I wished nonetheless to avoid any development of hard feelings. I couldn't fake a sudden illness (not good at that kind of thing) and had no credible way to obtain from friend or family news of a dire emergency requiring my presence elsewhere, so there seemed nothing to do but steel myself for the worst and join hosts and guests at the dinner table, which was where I found them congregated on my return to what I was now thinking of as the fray and where I found our number swelled by one, a young woman whose back was to me as I approached the table, the chair beside her being the only empty one, which I almost toppled when Black Satin turned with a smile of friendly politeness, in accompaniment to my host's introduction of her as Blackie. She was wearing a short black dress with frills at bodice and hem, her hair drawn up at the back and piled in artful disarray, a few stray wisps curling round her upper neck, below which rested a thin gold strand of necklace, a little gathering of gold bracelets ringing the slim wrist of her bare left arm, all of which I managed to take in despite the clenching of my stomach, the rush of blood to my head, the thickening of my tongue and of the thought processes that should have driven it to make some charming and complimentary opening remark, something to make memorable for her this moment of meeting, instead of "Oh, hello. Pleased to meet you," which was all I found myself capable of, and which yet proved adequate, providing me a base from which to build my self-composure, so that as the evening progressed, so did I, rising from a slough of fumble-tongued inadequacy to a level of urbane wit, intelligent comment, and generally entertaining, if not sparkling, conversational facility, sufficient, in any case, to make (I could tell) a favourable impression on Black Satin, from whom I managed to elicit appreciative laughter at various witticisms, serious consideration of points I made in opposition to some of the opinions offered by this or that person, and effusive agreement with my insights into one or two matters that came up for discussion in relation to the entertainment world. It wasn't surprising, then, that when the group as a whole broke from the dinner table to while away some time before dessert, restructuring itself in pairs or small groups of individuals with common interests or shared affinities, she and I found ourselves engaged in some discussion or other—of a movie we'd both recently seen and been impressed by, I believe, or else a play or a rock band, it doesn't really matter...the thing is we were getting along famously and found further common ground in our distaste for the "I Give Hugs" faction that seemed to encompass so many of our fellow diners, both of us wondering how our hosts, who we had always felt to be such genuine people, came to number among their friends these saccharine poseurs, one of whom (I think it was the female of the poets-beyond-publishing) insinuated herself into our conversation and at one point said, "So, Blackie, what do you do for a living?" the immediate response to which was "I'm a stripper." Silence. Which spread to the one or two conversations underway in our immediate vicinity. "Oh." Followed by an abrupt withdrawal. After a brief pause—during which Blackie turned to me, with, I thought, a rather challenging look in her eye, and I simply took up the thread of our discussion where it had dropped before the question was asked—the silenced conversations around us resumed and our hosts, soon after, hailed us to the dinner table for dessert. I found myself relieved that she obviously had no recollection of me as a hungry-eyed lecher at the various banquets of flesh in which she served herself. For my part, I refrained from asking why she never returned to dance with me at the Unzipped party, as she'd promised; and further, I found cause to congratulate myself on having brought off a full evening in her company without once losing myself in vividly imagined excesses of erotic indulgence with her, without seeing, in my mind's eye, the slow and delicious divestment of each article of her clothing, the gradual revelation of swelling breasts and firm buttocks, of soft loin and slim ankle, the welcoming spread of legs, the inflamed readiness of moist pudenda, the mouth slack with desire, the eyes widening with thrilled surprise at the sudden thrust of me within her, her arms pulling me tight against her, her fingers clutching at my head, threading through my hair, her little moans of pleasure and ecstatic scream in orgasm, the tender talk after making love, her finger tracing invisible designs across my chest while I cradle her in my arms and we mutter fondly into morning, which later finds us sleeping in the sun's strong rays, rising near noon for a breakfast of eggs and bacon and orange juice and "What a delicious trifle," said I-Give-Hugs, voicing his opinion around a mouthful of the confection he was praising, his enthusiasm finding echo in expressions voiced by all his fellow guests, whose spoons continued scraping and whose coffee cups kept clinking, creating a little symphony of praise to the culinary skills of our hostess, an image which I do not introduce just now in the act of writing about the event, as a kind of embellishment for the sake of telling a good story, but which occurred to me at the time and which led me to turn to Black Satin and ask if she was partial to Bartók (or maybe it was Dvorak or Prokoviev that I specified) and she asked, "Who?" and I passed on to a minor paean to the trifle, with which she concurred, things continuing pleasantly, liqueurs being served and cigarettes being smoked, conversation humming lazily about, until the first departures began to take their reluctant leave, and others found, soon after those first few announced their need to be off, a similar need, and one by one or two by two, our numbers dwindled, until none remained but our hosts and Blackie and me, and the frequency of yawns on everyone's part became a matter of comment and Blackie and I finally made our farewells, and I walked her to her car, where we lingered a bit in idle talk and I asked if I could see her again, would she give me her number, to which she responded by eyeing me briefly, looking away momentarily, then glancing down, her hand in her purse, withdrawing a card she held out to me, saying, "You can call me at that number," after which she got into her car, adding, as she closed the door, "And next time I have you do the routine with the licorice, don't lick."

6

It was in another city, a distant city, a city I had travelled to on business or for pleasure, I don't remember which, it doesn't matter, nothing matters, nothing mattered, except that it was there, in that city, that other city, on a coast or near a desert, I guess, except I'm sure it was a seaport, so it wouldn't have been near a desert, since seaports, I think, are rarely located near deserts, although it may have been on a river, where seaports often are, except that this one, I think, was not, but was on the ocean proper, I believe, if it's possible to believe me, not that I lie, god forbid—I don't do that, certainly not me—but I can be, often am, mistaken, and sometimes am mistaken for someone else, as once, I recall, the police mistook me for an armed bank robber, a type of person to whom they are not kind, believe me, if I can be believed, which I hope I can be and as, indeed, I should be, when I say that it was in another city, a distant city, a seaport, I think we can agree, although its exact location remains uncertain, because I either can't or won't remember, although whether it was near a desert or on a river or by the ocean itself, doesn't matter, nothing matters, nothing mattered, except that it was in that city so distant from the one in which we both lived that I saw her, where it would least be expected that she would be, by which I mean the city, the distant one—I mean it would least be expected that she would be there, in that city, to which I had travelled on business or for pleasure, I don't remember which, it doesn't matter, nothing matters, nothing mattered, except that she was there in that city where she would least be expected to be, by which I mean the city, not the place within it where she was, which was just the place she might well be expected to be, descending a ladder made of some kind of hard plastic with tiny flickering light bulbs set in the tubular rungs and squared uprights, the ladder leading down about eight feet from a square hatch in the ceiling to the floor of a raised stage, a small stage, by which I found myself sitting, looking expectantly up at the hatchway from which the short, precipitately slanted ladder descended, and on the top rung of which there appeared a tentative, slender, shapely foot, its spike-heeled slipper held on by a transparent plastic strap crossing at the ball of the foot and over, just at the start of the toes, their tiny several cleavages, their short elegant lengths, their nails painted a bright red, pale white stockings ascending her calves, which come into view beneath the hem of a loose white skirt as she makes her hesitant way down the ladder, balancing herself on the circular rungs with one hand sliding down the upright shaft inside which the tiny lights flicker, the other simultaneously clutching a flouncy, frilled white coverlet and holding tight the skirt about her legs, preventing any prying eye from peering up her dress to offend her modesty, as my eye wants to do, but being thus checked, gives itself over to an appraisal of the broad black patent-leather belt about her waist, that being the next item to come into view, followed by the white top of the dress with its upturned collar and the loops of a string of pearl-like beads about her shoulders and neck, as she sets herself upon the floor of the stage, drops her coverlet, and turns to survey her audience with a look of lightly mocking amusement, as though to say, "So you really do like this sort of thing, do you, you silly pups? Well, okay..." striding about, ignoring the beat of the music, apparently enjoying the rapt assessment given her fluffy blonde hairdo, her wide-set eyes, her pouting lips, her slender neck, her full bosom swelling within the loose bodice of her white dress that's held together by large black buttons, open at the neck and from the bottom to mid-thigh, her hands in the dress's capacious pockets, holding both sides of the skirt close to her legs and then slowly easing the sides apart, standing above me, smiling mischievously down, bending her knees in a developing crouch, revealing the opaque white stocking-tops and slender white garters that descend on either side of her absent panties, the pink beauty of her vulva protruding beneath her heart-shaped, tonsured blonde tuft, my eyes bulging, my breath coming short, my guts succumbing to a sag of desire, my stomach fluttering with nervous energy, all those states continuing throughout her performance, which has me puzzling over some several differences in her, things I hadn't noticed before, her figure fuller than I remembered, her breasts larger, her coloration fairer than it had previously seemed to me, her hair not the dark brown or black I was used to, her chin more rounded—little things, not that they matter, not that anything matters, not that anything mattered except that she was there, in that distant city, on that carpeted stage, rolling naked before me on her fluffy, frilled white coverlet or duvet, smiling amusedly at me, a thin film of sweat spangling her face, creating dew-like drops on the tiny blonde hairs that line her upper lip with its shiny red gloss, the long string of pearl-like beads unlooped from her neck and draped round her body, pulled tight at the crotch, buried in the moist folds of her genitals, where she plays it back and forth and then pulls it rapidly through, the small spheres flipping over her clitoris, as I lean forward further and say, semi-inquiringly, "Blackie...?" and she smiles, more politely than warmly, and I repeat, less inquisitively, "Blackie..." and she frowns with a little puzzled look and rolls over with a slight shrug and closes her eyes, their lids glistening with tiny drops of sweat or perhaps with sparkles in her blue eye shadow, and gives herself over, mouth agape in slack surrender to an ecstasy of orgasm that is either (I can't tell) real or simulated, not that it matters, nothing matters, nothing mattered, except that she was there, in a city where I would never have thought she would be, leaving the stage and later giving me a look of minor annoyance, as I approach her and say, "Nice show, Blackie," but don't press it, I can tell when I'm not welcome, can tell that she's protecting her true identity for some reason, though I can't imagine what one, she the only one that matters to me in this distant city or my own near one or any one, no one but her, who appears in my dreams that night, saying, "Silly pup, have you soaked your pants again? Mommy's told you what will happen if you don't use the newspaper. Silly pup, I'll have to spank you again...There!...a good swat should teach you yet...You'll learn sooner or later...Still not housebroken at your age...Bad dog!...Bad puppy!...Silly pup!" and I don't know why I dream these images, can't imagine why she approaches me with her black hair gray, her blonde hair wrapped in an old woman's kerchief, her face wrinkled like that of a woman I seem to remember, who is not my mother, who never smoked, the cigarette dangling from her mouth as she slaps me and screams, "How many times have I told you not to smoke? Just who do you think you are coming in here smoking cigarettes as though you were old enough to take your father's place?" and I say, "But I'm twenty-six! I'm thirty-three! I can so smoke! You said I could when I was sixteen! I don't want to take my father's place...I don't! I don't!"—don't want to hold that sour old bitch, screaming and hitting me, rotten old bag I don't want my arms around, pinched lips I don't want to kiss, full lips, trembling with sorrow at my father's death, straggly gray hair on balding old scalp I don't want to tenderly kiss and say, "It's all right...I'll look after you...You won't grow old abandoned...The best care, the best doctors..." as she weeps inconsolably, wrinkled breasts shaking against wrinkled belly inside her sad, worn housecoat, wailing, "How could he die?...Now when I need him?...What will I ever do here in a strange city?" my shirt wet with her tears, dreaming all this in a strange city, a distant city, a seaport perhaps...yes, certainly a seaport, whether near a desert or on a river or by an ocean, it doesn't matter, nothing matters, nothing mattered, except that she was here in this city where I never would have expected her to be, is in every city I am in, in none of which I expect her to be, in none of which she should be, in none of which she is, surely, not in any of them, dead these many years, descending a ladder made of some kind of hard plastic with tiny flickering light bulbs set in the tubular rungs and squared uprights, the ladder leading down about six feet from a rectangular hatch in the ceiling to the floor of a sunken stage, descending a ladder made of some kind of hard plastic with tiny flickering light bulbs set in the tubular rungs and squared uprights, the ladder leading down about eight feet from a square hatch in the ceiling to the floor of a raised stage, a small stage, by which I found myself sitting, looking expectantly up at the hatchway from which the short, precipitately slanted ladder descended, and on the top rung of which there appeared a tentative, slender, shapely foot, its spike-heeled slipper held on by a transparent plastic strap crossing at the ball of the foot and over, just at the start of the toes, their tiny several cleavages, their short elegant lengths, their nails painted a bright red, pale white stockings ascending her calves, which come into view beneath the hem of a loose white skirt as she makes her hesitant way down the ladder, balancing herself on the circular rungs with one hand sliding down the upright shaft inside which the tiny lights flicker, the other simultaneously clutching a flouncy, frilled white coverlet and holding tight the skirt about her legs, preventing any prying eye from peering up her dress to offend her modesty, as my eye wants to do, but being thus checked, gives itself over to an appraisal of the broad black patent-leather belt about her waist, that being the next item to come into view, followed by the white top of the dress with its upturned collar and the loops of a string of pearl-like beads about her shoulders and neck, as she sets herself upon the floor of the stage, drops her coverlet, and turns to survey her audience with a look of lightly mocking amusement, descending a ladder made of some kind of hard plastic with tiny flickering light bulbs set in the tubular rungs and squared uprights, the ladder leading down about six feet from a rectangular hatch in the ceiling to the floor of a sunken stage, a small stage, about eight feet by three feet, with an earthen floor, except, no, it's just a dark brown rug, a close-napped rug, so it looks like an earthen floor, though it's not an earthen floor by which I stand, looking down, my feet in the green grass around the rectangular hatch, I mean my feet in the green shag rug of the strip club, simulating grass so convincingly that I could believe I stand on grass by a rectangular hatch with a ladder descending at a precipitate angle, the ladder made of some kind of hard plastic with tiny flickering light bulbs set in the tubular rungs and squared uprights, up which ladder she climbs, clutching a ragged gray cover or sheet wound round her, reaching for me with bony hands, her eyes sunken and in shadow, glistening with moisture or tiny grains of rock powder from the sand, her eyes open now, her mouth agape, slack in surrender to the weight of her jaw, reaching for me from the frayed gray sheet that droops from her arms, reaching for me from the chill and musty air that surrounds her, reaching for me as the earth at my feet begins to crumble and I feel myself slipping towards her and scramble for my footing and gain solid ground that is sliding beneath me and shrink back, screaming, "Stay away from me! Stay away! You're dead! Go back! Do you hear me? You're dead! You're dead!" and wake up screaming, moist with chilling sweat and wrapped in a clammy sheet that is twisted about me in the gray morning of a seaport city, near a desert or on a river, or by an ocean, the city becoming visible outside the barely lightening rectangle of window on the far side of the hotel room, from which window descends, perpendicularly, the metal ladder of a fire escape, the drops of rain upon it picking up tiny reflections from the flickering light bulbs of the hotel sign.

7

The bar she suggested we meet at was in an old market section of town that was right around her place, she said, when she answered the call I'd put in to the number on her card, which number proved to be that of her booking agent, leading me to think that that would be an end of it: she wouldn't get the message or, getting it, would not respond; which, after four days, I was sure was the case, except that on the fifth day I heard from her, so I proposed dinner at a favourite restaurant of mine, an idea that she said sounded quite lovely, but her only free day was Sunday and it was already pretty busy and why didn't we just have a drink at this nice little third-worldy place she knew down in the market section near where she lived, which I of course agreed to, figuring, since it was so close to her place, that she might intend to have me walk her home after and it's only natural that she would invite me in for a coffee or cup of tea to kind of cut the alcohol for my drive home, an offer I'm only too willing to accept, charmed by her trim-lawned little house as we climb the steps to her front door, where she fumbles a little nervously for her key and we step inside the dim-lit hallway, helping each other out of our coats, getting them hung in the closet, and finding ourselves close to each other there in the narrow hall, her perfume alluring, her dress clinging to her voluptuous curves, my arm slipping easily, naturally, comfortably round her waist, as she relaxes into the embrace, the kiss, the caress, breaking briefly to say, "About that coffee..." but not bothering to pursue the matter, surrendering to the urge that is in us both, clutching at my ass as I clutch at hers, writhing in my arms and moaning, saying, just as I'm about to ask where the bedroom is, "Come on upstairs to the bedroom," where we hasten, at least as much as the feverish clinging and kissing we engage in on the way will allow, and, the bedroom once gained, she moves to a small cabinet, withdrawing two snifters and a bottle of cognac, saying, "We can have this; you won't be driving home tonight"—which, in another sense, I certainly wouldn't be, because, after she pulled up in her car outside the little third-worldy place, inside which I sat waiting, she announced, as she took the chair opposite me, that she was sorry, she could only stay a couple of hours at the most because her next job was out of town and she was driving there right after we'd had what she called our visit, so she could get some sleep in her hotel and be fresh for work the next day.

Not, I thought, an auspicious beginning. But a beginning nonetheless, I consoled myself: she had at least agreed to see me, which is more than could be said of a number of other previous such fascinations—women admired from afar, seen regularly either in business or social settings, in neighbourhood shops or in bars I frequented, seen until some familiarity is established and pleasantries escalate to conversations that turn into discussions that lead to invitations that meet with rejections, which was how I took her relegating our meeting to a brief interim appointment between whatever she had scheduled that day and her departure to an outlying town that evening, sort of like a concession to some wilful child making onerous demands on a parent, although I certainly didn't feel like a child in relation to her (the kind of demands I had in mind hardly being the type that a child would make), despite the fact that I did feel a bit petulant about her not wanting to spend more time with me, which was petty of me, I must admit, since she did agree to see me and maybe even made a hole in her busy schedule to accommodate our getting together, however briefly, probably cancelling some engagement out of fear that I might not bother to contact her again if she didn't see me this first time ("Listen," I imagined her saying to some girlfriend or guy, "something's come up and I can't make it tonight, but I'll get in touch when I'm back in town, okay? Really sorry, but this is pretty important"), except I figured it was more likely that she'd decided I was a pest and she'd squeeze in this one appointment to use as a means of discouraging me, ridding herself of me once and for all, trumping up some story about leaving town, then going off to spend the night with her latest lover, unless, of course, she had a lover waiting for her in the town she was going to, whatever town that was, which I never did find out, since every time I went to ask her about it we got off on some other topic, most often something related to her painting, which she was quite serious about, working very hard at it apparently, taking art courses, fixing up a studio in the house she'd just put a down payment on with the good money she was earning as a headliner on the strip circuit, which led her to refer with scorn to the bimbos (she called them) who blew everything on drugs or booze and wound up with nothing to show for it all once they got too old or burnt-out to keep dancing, a reality she was not going to blind herself to but was saving up against, planning a couple of other things as well that she could fall back on in case she never made it as a painter, which it intrigued me to learn that she was striving towards, art being a subject I knew a bit about, so that I drew her out on the topic of her work and we discussed our respective tastes, discovering a shared enthusiasm for Rothko, a shared dislike of Appel, and a difference of opinion on Lichtenstein, whose work she loved, even though it wasn't at all a style she was personally interested in, especially right now when she was concentrating on classic figure work, establishing a basis in skills that she intended to develop in a very different direction, but which I figured would mean that she might, at least at some point, need a little help in the way of a male model who wouldn't charge for sitting, content to endure the drafts and chilly air that invade the poorly insulated studio while she labours over capturing the exact slope of shoulder or curve of buttock, asking me to shift my position just a bit so she can get a better view of my genitals, passing the occasional compliment on my legs or buns or pecs, smiling and saying it was getting kind of hard to concentrate on her work and anyway we should take a break, I'd probably like a beer after sitting there for so long in the sweltering heat, she was so sorry she couldn't afford air conditioning for hot days like this and, oh, I needn't bother putting any clothes on for the break—it was so hot, and anyway, she kind of liked having me that way; here...I could just sit on the couch beside her and even though it was an awfully sticky night she hoped I wouldn't mind that she couldn't resist running her fingers through the hairs on my chest and maybe just licking a bit at my nipple there, as I give a tiny gasp of pleasure at the expert application of tongue and lips, which find their way to other parts of my body, where tongue and lips have their work met with the kind of response that she wants, that we both want, as she's all over me and tugging her tight jeans down while I remove the flimsy blouse that has been almost transparent with the moisture of our mixed sweat, and I am inside her, both of us shuddering our way to satisfaction, her saying after, "I don't think it was a good idea to use you as a model...I can hardly get any painting done," smiling as she wipes the beads of sweat from my brow, snuggling up against me to lend me warmth in the shivering cold of the studio I certainly wouldn't be seeing tonight, sitting talking with her in her third-worldy bar filled with third-worldy men who gave her the once-over time and again, while I responded to her questions about my work and my lifestyle, saying no, I didn't have any children, did she? at which her expression lost some of the guarded look that had characterized it to that point and she lowered her eyes, saying, "Not exactly..." and I asked if she meant she'd adopted one, wondering about a husband hovering in the background, soon to be disclosed, but she said that no, what she meant was, well...and since it was obviously something touchy I told her it was okay if she didn't want to say, I was only asking out of curiosity, not to pry, but she said it wasn't prying, it was no big deal any more, it was just that she'd once been pregnant and had lost the kid. That stopped me short. I wondered if it was recent, but didn't want to ask, so merely expressed my sympathy for the grief it must have caused her and she thanked me, brushing the matter aside, saying it was okay, she was over it, and we went back to discussing art or movies or, in any case, something else, I don't remember what, but do remember her occasional look of distraction, which, in other circumstances I might have taken personally, as a sign of disinterest in me, but which I figured was probably the result of her thinking back to her loss, the knowledge of which made me feel pissed off at the lustful looks the patrons of the place were directing towards her, thinking to myself, You bastards...here's a woman who's had a tragedy to contend with and all you can think of is how much you'd like to lay her, which, as I think of it, I guess I couldn't blame them for, since they had no way of knowing, really, and even though I did, I must admit I couldn't remove all such thoughts from my mind, however secondarily I felt them at that point and later, still, as we were saying good night to each other on the empty Sunday-night street, the market no longer teeming with the life that had filled it the day before, when the shops overflowed their bins and bushels onto the crowded sidewalks now bare before the dark windows and locked doors, a light mist of spring rain, I think, sprinkling the road and the two of us in the chill evening—it was a chill evening, I remember, though whether in spring or fall I guess I really couldn't say, the weather being the kind that might occur in either of those seasons or even on a mild winter night, with the misty precipitation mixing raindrops and snow: light, wet snow that landed moistly on our cheeks, the two of us standing outside her little third-worldy tavern near the vacant playground, saying we'd get together again, I'd call her when she got back to town if I didn't have to leave on business myself in the meantime, which was prone to happen around that time of year, whichever it was, early spring or late fall I think, when the evenings are chill and the old market has a desolate, deserted air about it and there is apt to be rain or a light snow, such as there was that night, one or the other, rain I think, though so fine as to be almost a fog or mist, creating a thin film of moisture on her car, beside which she stood, her keys in hand, the mist or snow or rain or fog shining faintly on her hair in the rays of the streetlight overhead, her expression pensive, maybe even a little wistful, looking off in some other direction, as I suggest another meeting when she's back in town or we're both back, since I sometimes get called away unexpectedly on some urgent matter or other, but it might be nice to take in a few exhibits at some of the small galleries if we can find a day when we're both free, at which she nods once or twice with a little smile, saying, "Sure," and getting into her car, pulling away, as I give a little wave and hunch my shoulders against the cold, walking through the old market, past the silent shops, a few empty wooden counters obtruding onto the sidewalk, little white wisps of snow sifting over them in the wind.

8

She began more and more to occupy my thoughts, so that I
might be observed, say, at a filing cabinet, bending over at the
waist a bit to hide the precipitate bulge sprung in my pants by
the unbidden image of her breasts or buttocks or lips or eyes
or face or figure...and sometimes not even an image, but just
her name popping into my mind or even the mere suggestion
of her name, as when, once, a meeting I was in revolved
around the prudence of spending extra to have a promotion-
al item printed on a fancy paper called "Satincoat Gloss,"
which name was repeated incessantly throughout the meeting,
conjuring her image continually before me, so that it
behooved me to linger behind, making a show of tying my
shoelaces...except no, I had loafers on and my delaying tactic
was the feigned discovery of a bothersome stone or stones in
one or both of my shoes, unless I had perhaps found it necessary to adjust my socks, although I suspect that it was probably all of these—socks, stones, and shoelaces—that I called on
as excuses for staying seated and bent over, while my superior
hurried me and chided me for needlessly holding up the

impatient next group that waited to use the meeting room, hovering outside while my hard-on persisted, as it sometimes does when I don't need it and sometimes doesn't when I do, until finally it subsided and I departed, properly socked and unpebbled and (if it wasn't just loafers I had on) laced—and more than a little red-faced into the bargain; not, of course, that anyone attendant on the incident would be aware of the real reason for my dawdling departure (or would they?), but my own awareness was enough to ignite a blush in my cheeks, even without the curious and less than friendly attention that my untoward lingering had attracted from the assembled and inconvenienced group.

Bad enough that I surrendered to her, in exponential increments, the territory of my daily thoughts—that much, I had long since learned, came with the territory when these kinds of fascination were upon me, although I usually gained at least some of the territory back after getting to know the object of my dubious affections and finding her accessible in whatever degree, let alone going out with her as much as I was with Blackie, who accepted my invitations to dinner and to gallery openings, and even extended invitations to me, suggesting I turn up at this or that friend's showing at one gallery or another; bad enough, I say...but, in addition, I found myself still with an insatiable appetite for viewing her public disrobings, the pending location of which I determined by poring regularly over the strip-club ads in the sleazy local tabloid or, if she was not among the headliners at the clubs that advertised during any given week, embarking on voyages of discovery to as many of the unadvertised clubs as I was able to get to until (and if) I got to the one where she was working, an enterprise that entailed dispensing with the pursuits of any hobbies for which I might have events scheduled that week, skipping meals (or ingesting the execrable slop that passed for food in the strip joints), rearranging my schedule, cancelling social engagements that seemed worthwhile when I set them up but proved eminently expendable in light of the prospect of examining once more the supple litheness of her diminutive form, the smooth, unblemished expanse of her skin, the moist, inviting softness of her vulva, her legs draped over my shoulders, limp in surrender to the erotic ecstasy evoked in her by my accomplished lingual and manual ministrations, the gradual tensing that presaged her coming and that began, I could sense, though not perceive, in her toes, which no doubt straightened and pulled together as the sensation built, the tension progressing through her feet, which pointed and curled inwards as she tensed her calves, straightened her knees, clenched her thighs, arched her spine, tightened the muscles of her belly and lower back, and gave herself over to a shuddering, thrashing, hip-pounding, screaming, volcanic multiple orgasm, looking at me after with urgent, grateful, eagerly loving eyes, tearing herself regretfully away from me to sweep from the distant stage, a focal point I always made sure to keep myself well back from, witnessing her shows now only at a discreet distance, taking every possible precaution to avoid being seen by her—sitting at a table well-removed from the stage and the dressing-room door, wearing dark glasses whenever she was not onstage, huddling in my chair if she was strolling around the club floor—because, having become acquainted with her, something in my mentality reversed, and where I previously had done all in my power to draw her attention to me as she peeled off her clothes, a kind of reverse modesty set in and I was embarrassed at the prospect of watching the woman I was taking to dinner on Sunday or a speakeasy on Friday easing out of her garments and rolling around in the nude while I sat there sipping beer and smiling up at her.

It was towards the end of an evening I'd spent in one such search, which had proved futile, that I found myself parked at a table in some suburban joint populated by peaked-capped patrons, with half-clad girls roaming the floor in search of customers to table dance for, when one of the girls caught my fancy as she sashayed by and I decided to indulge myself in a little private show, more out of boredom than anything else, a kind of whimsical consolation for having failed to succeed in the evening's aim, so I hailed her and she fetched her stool—a little portable platform, not unlike the kind used as perches for circus seals—returning with it to my table and positioning it near me, sitting down on it till the song in progress ended, making small talk and laughing (a little nervously, I thought), then mounting the low stool, tall and a bit ungainly, rather plump but nonetheless appealing, dancing half-heartedly as she undid her bra, which she wore under a loose, open, oversized white blouse—more like a man's dress shirt, actually—removing the strapless bra while keeping the blouse on, all of which I took as part of the tease, until she said, with self-conscious laugh and embarrassed demeanour, "Look at my *eyes*," at which I thought, What's wrong with them? but did as I was asked, while she tugged her blouse or shirt around her capacious bosom and reached down to pull off her panties, her legs squeezed modestly together, me asking, "Why your eyes?" to which she gave a sighing little half-

laugh, a big sheepish smile on her face, saying, "I just...well—
guys never look at anything but my *body* all the time and it
just...well, it *bothers* me," to which I had no reply, too busy
wondering why she was involved in this line of work if she felt
that way, which seemed too large an issue to take up right
then, so that finally, she being so obviously uncomfortable
with the whole enterprise, I told her it was okay, she didn't
have to dance or take off her clothes if she didn't want to, at
which she beamed with delight, thanking me while tugging
her panties on, declining my offer to pay for the table dance
anyway, then looking at me studiously and asking, "Were you
at a big party called Unzipped?" upon my acknowledgement
of which she said, "I think I met you there," and indeed, I recognized her then as the lady who had been behind me during
Black Satin's performance that night, and said, "Yes, I believe
we did sort of meet," and she settled down on her stool and
started talking about the party, from which she moved on to
telling me everything from her troubles with her boyfriend ("I
keep my place clean, so why can't he? I mean, I hate a hairy
bathroom, y'know?") to what she'd had for breakfast that day
(banana bread and fruit salad, if memory serves me right),
pausing for a moment to order drinks for us both ("On me,"
she insisted) from a passing waitress, before continuing with an
account of her plans for the future ("I want to be a dance ther-
apist") and her intentions for the present ("I make a lot more
money doing this than I could ever make in a regular job"),
so that before I know it, they're closing the bar and she's saying, "Oh, you have a car?! I was going to call for a cab, but..."
and again before I know it, I'm offering to drive her home and
she's inviting me in for a coffee and her plump legs are not the

graceful limbs of my devoutly desired Black Satin, but they are
around my neck and then around my hips and I am happy for
a moment, lost in the straining conjunction of two moaning,
heaving, gasping, grunting, clutching, scrambling, stiff-nippled,
soft-twatted, hard-cocked human beings, slippery with sweat
and saliva and cunt juice and come, during which I remember
thinking, as my fingers delved her soaked sheath and my
tongue and teeth flicked and nibbled at first one nipple and
then the other, how unlike Black Satin she was, whose breasts
were smaller and firmer, belly flatter, ankles slimmer, eyes
brighter, flesh darker, my legs draped over her shoulders, limp
in surrender to the erotic ecstasy she evokes in me with puck-
ered lips and busy tongue, head of red hair lifting and dropping there, lifting and dropping, an occasional rude slurp or
unladylike snort escaping from behind the curtain of blonde
tresses that rise and fall at my belly, as first one flattened palm
and then the other feather against the hair of my balls, the
merest hint of contact between her flesh and mine, then the
gradual tensing that presages my coming and that begins, she
can sense, though not perceive, in my toes, which no doubt
straighten and pull together as the sensation builds, the tension
progressing through my feet, which point and curl inwards as
I tense my calves, straighten my knees, clench my thighs, arch
my spine, tighten the muscles of my belly and lower back, and
give myself over to a surging, spastic, thrusting, body-tingling
ejaculation in the self-and-time-obliterating eruption of
orgasm, my fulfillment in which I trumpet to the world with
what begins as a deep-throated moan and swells and loudens
to a soaring howl of exhilarated release, after which I lie slack
and spent and drifting lazily in and out of sleep, her head on

my chest, my face buried in her soft black curls, whose odour
I find uniquely consoling, an olfactory cloud on which I float
in post-coital languor, vaguely aware of her breathing, her finger tracing little circles in the hairs on my chest, which is how
I find her again (or still) when I waken in sunlight and pull
myself reluctantly out of bed to make my slow and tardy way
to work, leaving her to sleep the morning till her afternoon
and nighttime work begins again and I set out on another
search of suburban and ex-urban clubs for the one Black
Satin's in that week, hunting through a forest of erotically
evocative names—Midnight Lace and Misty Tease, Velvet
Dream and Magie Noire, Temptation, Godiva, Angel Eyes,
Cynthia Peel, Chiffon Tart, Sheri De Lite, Lustana, Honey
Fire, Sugar Cream—under a rain of less exotic appellations—
Debbies and Dawns, Roses, Lauras, Ericas, Chantels, Suzies,
Sharons, Bonnies, Brandys, Brigittes, Michelles and Lindas,
Anns and Suzettes, until I find myself outside a place that
advertises Sweet Satin or Black Velvet or Satin Dream, and
entertain the irrational hope that it is her with a slight modu-
lation in name, effected for whatever reason, perhaps to throw
me off her track, though she surely couldn't have known I was
on it, since I'd taken every conceivable precaution to see that
she didn't, even going so far as never to appear for our dates
in the same clothes I wore when I made the rounds of the
clubs, of which there were more than I'd have thought one
metropolitan area could support, places with names like The
Top-Hat, Sheers, Pink Pussy-Cat, Garter and Stocking, Hot
Licks, Bunny-O's, Candy's, and -er's by the dozen: Cutter's,
Clipper's, Keeper's, Flasher's—a composite cornucopia spilling
priestesses of lust across altars fringed with strips of flickering

bulbs, washed by soft beams of red and blue and yellow and green, lit by the garish flash of strobes, presided over by the pastor of the P.A., who exhorts the faithful from his sound-booth pulpit to "Get the best seat in the house—take your pick of our gorgeous girls and have her dance for you right at your table for just a few dollars" and to "Come on, guys, get your hands out of your pockets and put them together to show this luscious lady how much you appreciate her," sermons I largely ignored, busy calculating the number of strip joints I could get to that night, mentally mapping a route that would cover a maximum of clubs with a minimum of travel, indifferent to all that transpired around me, alert only to that which might point to the prospect of seeing Black Satin, who exerted such control over me, whether or not she intended it, that I might as well have been on a collar and leash, my movements dictated by where she was or might possibly be, first tugged here, then yanked over there, pulled inside this place, left outside that one, curtailing my will in deference to hers, perhaps initially straining towards this or that contrary point, but soon giving in to obedient, willing, joyful submission, eager to lap at her heels and lick her feet, to roll over, run and fetch, sit up and beg, grateful for any sign of affection: a scratch behind the ears, a pat on the head, a little biscuit or extended petting, extra food in my bowl or a heartfelt "Good boy! Oh what a good boy you are! Ohhhhhh yes, yes, yes..." spoken while holding my snout in both hands and playfully shaking my head back and forth till my body wags as I make mental note of the behaviour that elicited so favourable a response, whatever it might have been that I'd done, a clever trick perhaps—such as catching in mid-air a ball that was tossed to me,

jumping and twisting and taking it in my teeth, running back
to her to lay it at her feet and look up at her with hopeful,
expectant eyes—or maybe the correct execution of some
order or command that had previously proved beyond my
capacity...something like that, anything like that, whatever I
could do to earn some reward, no matter how trifling, always
trying to anticipate and, if possible, fulfill her desires, do for her
what she wanted me to or what I believed she wanted me to,
all the time wondering if she knew her power over me, hoping she did, sure that she must, wishing she'd exercise it, wanting to have her boss me around, set me difficult tasks and punish my failures with disapproving remarks and withheld
embraces, place demands on me, however unreasonable, have
me scrub her walls and tidy her rooms, make her meals and
tend her grounds, confine me to the house for days at a time
without clothing or money so I couldn't go out, insist I wash
her panties in the laundry of my mouth, wake me in the middle of the night to flaunt her nakedness before me, uttering
stern commands to touch neither her nor myself, as I lie there
erect and immobile and she leers and lasciviates, tying me
down to ensure my compliance, masturbating with a carrot or
zucchini before feeding it to me, having me sit on one side of
a subway car, facing the aisle, wearing tight pants and no
underwear, while she sits directly opposite in a low-cut dress
with a short skirt, pretending not to know me as she repeatedly leans forward and crosses and uncrosses her legs so that I
see down her dress and up her skirt, and my stiffened cock,
clearly defined within the straining fabric of my pants, is obvious to all the nearby passengers, who variously snicker, smirk,
glare in disgust, or move away with angry expressions, after

which she takes me home and makes me serve her and her girlfriends at a formal party where they are seductively dressed and I am clad only in a bowtie and tiny apron that ends just above my untameable hard-on, which I am neither to touch nor have touched and which pulses unbearably under the constant gaze of hostess and guests till it finally spatters its white cargo on the carpet and I am instructed to get down on all fours and lick it up, an occurrence that transpires two or three times in the course of the evening, an evening I beg to have repeated and which she tells me several times is arranged and each time tells me—after I spend days cleaning and polishing the whole house in eager anticipation of the pending ordeal—is cancelled. But I wouldn't hear of anything sick or perverted, no matter how much she might try to subject me to being walked on, pissed on, made to fish out her turds from the toilet and smear myself with them, rubbing my cock with her shit till I come, nothing as vile or extreme as that, which anyway she would never do, having too much respect for me, not wanting to control me, I not wanting to be controlled by her, both of us wanting only to love and to be loved, performing the little services and treats that lovers delight in favouring each other with: breakfast in bed, a rose picked up on the way home from work as a gift before a concert, a special meal prepared as a surprise, a spontaneous show of affection in a public place, a bracelet, necklace, or other extravagance purchased on whim, help with finances, advice on handling people or situations, counsel and consolation, material aid and emotional support, sudden eruptions of passion in the kitchen, where dinner is abandoned in impulsive surrender to physical urges, thoughtful little gifts of negligee or underthings, considerate calls to avoid inconvenience when this or that plan must be surrendered to some professional exigency, kindness and fairness the order of the day, with no sexual power playing, no emotional manipulation, no embarrassment in front of a friend that she has to lunch, a statuesque blonde wearing skimpy cut-offs without any underpants and a flimsy blouse that barely contains her bra-less and melon-like breasts and whose visit I've been prepared for by not being permitted any sexual outlet for two weeks (my clothing and bedding scrupulously inspected throughout that time to ensure against surreptitious masturbation, left not a moment's privacy, forbidden to close the bathroom door and subjected to unannounced scrutiny there), so I'm excessively horny, but have been issued strict instructions not to ogle the guest, who, however, at one point, with a forkful of food halfway to her mouth, stops and announces, in outraged tone, "Blackie! He's staring at my tits! And he's got a great big hard-on!" at which Blackie puts down her wineglass, directs her gaze to the unmistakable bulge in my pants, pushes back her chair, motions for me to come over to her and asks quietly, "Do you like her tits?" and I hang my head and keep silent, which leads her to say, "You answer me when I talk to you!...Do you like her tits?" "Y-y-yes," I stammer, swelling even more and trembling in anticipation of what might transpire. "So you must have looked at them." Silence. "What did I tell you earlier?" I swallow and say, "Not to ogle your guest." "But you've been doing just that, haven't you?" Considering the question rhetorical, I maintain my silence, at which she slaps my face and says, "Answer me!" so I whimper and mumble yes, to which she says, "Answer as though you had some balls, for Christ's sake!" and, in my peripheral vision,

I can see the blonde's amused little smile and notice her leaning forward and pulling her arms slightly together so that her breasts almost spill from her blouse. "Yes," I say, loudly and clearly, "I was looking at her tits." "Did you have a good look?" Blackie asks, with mock solicitation. "No. Just a glance." "Oh," she responds facetiously, continuing in iron-edged tone with, "but I suppose you'd like a good long look, wouldn't you?" thereby putting me on the spot, since the admission of such a desire would be a breach of etiquette and an insult to the guest, yet to deny it would be to contradict Blackie and still insult the guest by implying that her tits aren't attractive, so that I pause in momentary confusion, which draws a quietly threatening "Answer me," at which I decide to risk a "Yes." "Well," says Blackie, again in facetious tone, "maybe she'll give you just that. Debbie?" Without a word, but with an evidently suppressed smile, Debbie removes what little there is of her blouse as I stand with head hung until Blackie says scornfully, "She's showing you her tits. Look at them," and I direct my gaze to the large, smooth, pink-tipped spheres that Debbie displays, rising from her chair and standing close in front of me, cupping her breasts with her hands and lifting them towards me, pinching and pulling her nipples until they stand erect, scant inches from my eyes. "Now what about her ass and her cunt?" asks Blackie in mocking tone. "Don't you want to see them, too?" "Oh please," I beg, swallowing hard and trembling with desire, hearing Blackie inquire, "Deb?" and Debbie saying, "Sure. Why not? Little boys have to have their little fun, don't they?" sliding the zipper of her cut-offs down as Blackie pushes my head level with Debbie's crotch and her tonsured blonde tuft comes into view and she turns around, easing the

denim cloth over the lush globes of her ass, her shorts dropping to the floor as she pulls her cheeks apart and runs a slender finger, its nail painted red, over the pinkish-brown flesh of
her asshole and down to spread the lips of her damp cunt,
whose rich aroma swirls in my nostrils, as I moan and breathe
heavily, rampant with arousal, hearing Blackie say, with contrived resignation and regret, "But I told you not to ogle my
guest and here you are staring and panting and almost cream-
ing your jeans. I'm afraid I have no choice but to punish
you..." (all while holding my head at Debbie's crotch, where
the voluptuous blonde is working two fingers in and out of
her twat in slow masturbation, the pungent odour driving me
mad with desire) "...I'm sorry, but I'm going to have to ask
you to take your pants down," an instruction I follow without
changing position, stepping out of my trousers, the only thing
I've been allowed to have on, which done, Blackie grips my
hair and pulls back my head, turning me towards her, saying
with impatience, "Get these clothes off me! How do you
expect me to administer proper punishment with these things
on?" and I remove her blouse and slacks, her bra and panties,
quivering with fear and arousal, wincing with pain as she tugs
at my hair, saying, "Hurry up! We haven't got all day," and then,
"Debbie, I'm really sorry things turned out like this. He's been
so good the last few days. I was sure he'd behave himself while
you were here, and now he's gone and ruined it all. Look, it
must be embarrassing for you. You don't have to stay and
watch this if you don't want to." But Debbie replies that no,
she thinks it might be a lesson to me if someone is there from
outside the household who disapproves of my behaviour just
as much as Blackie does—maybe it will embarrass me into

changing my ways, during which remarks Blackie has resumed her chair, keeping a firm grip on my hair, while Debbie, fighting to maintain a stern and disapproving expression, arranges herself in a chair to the left of Blackie, slouching down with her heels on the edge of the seat so that when Blackie yanks me down across her knees, still holding my head back by the hair, my face is almost buried in the slippery folds of Debbie's cunt and my bursting member pulses with tiny spasms as it pokes down between Blackie's thighs, the right one of which my balls brush against, while the left is prodded by my persistently throbbing rod, and I see, by forcing my eyes up towards Debbie's face, that she is peering down and around so that her gaze falls on the point where I know my erection shows below Blackie's soft, dark-tanned thigh and, at the same moment, out of the corner of my eye I see Blackie's free hand reach across to grasp the handle of the paddle-shaped plastic cheeseboard, at which I lower my gaze to see both of Debbie's hands at her crotch, the left cupping her buttock in such a way that the pad of her middle finger reaches to her asshole, where she pats with it and makes little circles, the right pressed down between her legs and over her box, where her fingers rub her labia and plunge into the soaked interior as the first stinging swat from Blackie's cheeseboard paddle strikes my buttocks, causing me to involuntarily press downwards with my hips, increasing the contact between my genitals and Blackie's thighs, which she squeezes lightly together just at that point, then eases them apart, shifting her position a bit between the first and the second spank, during which interval I feel the barest touch of her wet cunt and wiry pubic hairs before the second spank strikes and the friction repeats, as it continues to do with each stroke, after about four of which Debbie observes that "You'd think a boy who'd been so naughty and who was getting such a spanking would cry a little bit if he was really sorry for what he'd done, wouldn't you, Blackie?" to which Blackie replies, "Oh, he'll cry all right," increasing the force and rapidity of the strokes, and I do squeeze out some tears and howl a lot, not because it hurts so much, since my bum is so numb I can hardly feel it, but because Debbie wants me to and I want to please her because she's Blackie's friend and to please her is to please Blackie and I would do anything to please Blackie, screaming and crying and watching Debbie's soaking fingers thrusting in and out of her vagina and flipping over her clitoris till her legs tense and the motion of her fingers increases in speed and intensity so that I know that she's coming and the bouncing I'm doing in Blackie's lap is harder and faster, me all slippery with pre-ejaculate fluid and Blackie's cunt juice, till finally my come spurts out between her legs and onto the floor, at which I hear Debbie laugh, her laughter continuing as I'm made to get down and lick up my mess, some of it all over Blackie's feet, how careless of me, oh shame, shame on lucky, licking me, who rolls on the floor to more easily suck at the soft, sweet sole of Blackie's right foot, my head pressed into the kitchen tile as she pushes her foot down hard against my mouth and Debbie laughs and laughs, making me so glad that I've given such pleasure to a friend of Blackie's, looking up happy and hoping for approval from Blackie, whose heel I'm trying to get all inside my mouth, her helping me so kindly by pushing hard to get it in there and making me so happy by smiling—I can see her smiling—looking over at Debbie and joining her in

laughing, making me feel so lucky to be able to do anything
to make Blackie happy, but nothing sick or perverted, nothing
like letting her walk on me, punish me, hit me or hurt me,
unable to even think of anything like that, not knowing why
I did, not wanting anything like that, upset that such things
could even cross my mind, not that they did, not that I'd let
them, not that I'd ever say if they did, not that I'd let Blackie
know, not that it would matter to her, not that she knew the
power she had over me, not that she would use it if she did,
wouldn't be unkind, wouldn't hit me, wouldn't hurt me,
wouldn't shame or debase me, not that I'd want her to, not that
I'd ever want any woman to, not knowing what it's like to be
hurt by a woman, never having been hurt by a woman, not
physically, not cruelly, not any woman, not even my mother,
who only punished me for my own good, being otherwise
kind, being understanding, being patient when finding me
smearing my feces all over myself and rubbing my infant cock
with my shit, which did not send her into paroxysms of rage,
did not cause her to hit me or hurt me, screaming and uttering sounds of disgust, slapping my hands when they strayed
towards my penis, complaining to guests of my misbehaviour,
exerting her power over me, tugging me here, yanking me
there, pulling me into one store, leaving me in my carriage
outside another, subjugating my will completely to hers,
though I strained initially towards this or that contrary point,
soon realizing the futility of physical opposition and giving in
to whimpering, crying, howling, not because it hurt so much,
but because she would then pick me up and hold me, hug me
and kiss me, saying, "Ohhhh, there's a good boy...yeeees, what
a good boy...that's mummy's good boy," kissing me wetly and

hugging me closely, bringing me pablum, holding a flower for me to sniff, its heady odour swirling through my nostrils, offering me a pacifier, kissing me suddenly outside a store, buying a trinket for me just on whim, helping with finances, advising on handling people or situations, giving counsel and consolation, material aid and emotional support, erupting in sudden rage at a lapse in my table manners, food forgotten in an impulsive tirade, confining me to my room for swearing or smoking, refusing to talk to me for days on end, only breaking her silence to make disapproving remarks, withholding her embraces, looking hurt and surly, relenting some when I bring her breakfast in bed or clean the house, wash the dishes or take out the garbage, warming a bit when I sacrifice my allowance to buy her a bracelet or box of chocolates, a flower perhaps or a string of beads, the little services and treats that lovers delight in favouring each other with, wanting only to love and be loved.

9

While we were in bed once—we had begun to go to bed together on occasion, though not for the longest time, "the longest time" to me being anything beyond immediately, especially since she, while not going to bed with me, would sleep around with any number of one-time lovers and long-time friends, either of which category I was eager to qualify for and said so, only to be told that we obviously were too recently acquainted to be long-time anything, but that I had already come to mean more to her than just a casual fling, and that she valued me as a friend, though not, I reflected, a long-time friend, wondering how long it took to be so classified and watching her stroll away again with another lover, which should not be taken to mean that she was capricious: I don't want to misrepresent her; however much she may come across that way in this account, it is, after all, only my account and therefore not reliable as absolute truth, even though I am being as truthful as I can be, which I hope is truthful enough, although truthful enough for what, I can't say, I don't know, though I hope I might sometime, which I suspect will be the longest time, which was the length of time, it seemed, that she wouldn't go to bed with me but would go to bed with countless others, out of grief, I think, because she mentioned to me that she'd recently gone through a very painful breakup, maybe even a divorce, I don't remember, I can't say, I don't know, although she did talk about it at length and in detail and I paid close attention and was very commiserative, which was how I felt, even though I don't remember all the details, probably because I wanted to go to bed with her so badly: I can't say, I don't know, I just know that he was the guy who had gotten her pregnant and they broke up a few years after she lost the kid and when she told me about it she became very distraught at one point, crying and saying, "How could he leave me?...I needed him so badly!" (or was it "I need him so badly!"?), my shirt wet with her tears, her firm breasts shaking within the silk blouse she wore without a bra or perhaps with a push-up one that accentuated the fullness of her bosom, as she wept in my arms and I thought how this would surely bring me closer to the category of long-time friend, if not in actual temporal terms, then in terms of intimacy, which should count for something in these kinds of things, and I couldn't take my eyes off the purple silk of her blouse and the full swell of her breasts shaking beneath it, chastising myself all the time for having a hard-on when she was pouring out her grief, but unable to ignore the stimulating warmth of her body through the smooth fabric of her blouse against my hand at her waist, the fragrance of her hair beneath my nose, the pressure of her hand on my shoulder, the sight of her thighs as her skirt crept up her legs, and I wondered if maybe I was a sadist, taking some perverse delight in her pain, although I felt keenly her sense of loss and my heart went out to her, even more another time, when I learned that she had lost her father shortly after her relationship went all to hell, so I can understand how she might become promiscuous, I mean because of the breakup, not because of her father's death, which it obviously wouldn't make sense for it to have that kind of effect, but when a serious affair ends it's easy to see that she'd want to satisfy her physical urges without any emotional involvement, which anyone might do for a time, myself included, although I'd never been involved with anyone as heavily as she'd been with the guy she told me about that time when she wore the purple silk blouse without a bra or with a push-up one that accentuated the rich swell of those soft globes and her black skirt kept creeping up her bare legs, revealing the tawny flesh of her thighs, at the top of which, I guess, she was snugged into some frilly white panties, or maybe purple ones to match her blouse, I don't know, I can't say, I never saw.

Anyway, while we were in bed once, after we'd begun sleeping together on occasion, and I was busy paying homage to her posterior, which she'd raised before me by tipping forward on her knees so that I was presented with a lush banquet of private parts that I approached with grateful reverence, first softly caressing the twin swells, then nuzzling and nestling against them with my cheeks, running my tongue between them, licking delicately at the sensitive dark flesh of her asshole as I moved one hand down to lightly touch the lips of her vulva, pressing my mouth now with more fervour round the tight little opening I so eagerly stimulated, hearing her moan with sighing pleasure as I applied a rapid sequence of gentle little sucking kisses and probed with insistent tongue, lavishing one last luxurious kiss there before moving on to the soft, moist folds of her vulva, spreading her lips and lapping repeatedly, stopping occasionally to flick my tongue over the swelling bud of her clitoris, lapping again and flicking, one or two busy fingers inserted into the damp, warm interior, plunging and rubbing and pressing and wriggling, while she responded with a gratifying little concert of sighs and moans and gasps and a proliferating stream of vaginal fluid, her fingers squeezing and pulling her nipples, her face pressed sideways against the sheets, rocking gently and sighing, "Oh, love me," which surprised me a bit because I thought that was what I was doing and I remember pausing briefly amid my ministrations to wonder why she would say that and feeling foolish then as I continued, realizing that it was doubtless simply an encouragement to me, from the depths of her arousal, to carry on with what I was doing, for which I needed no urging, but then I thought perhaps she might have meant that she was ready for me to enter her and so I began to withdraw my mouth and fingers until she said, "Oh, please keep doing that...it feels so good," and I returned to the task with added fervour, the ultimate result being a mighty tensing on her part and then a thrashing and a long, shuddering cry as she experienced the release of orgasm, then rolled over and guided me into her, crying out at the peak of our activity, "Oh, fuck me! Yes! Love me!" and it was later that I began to consider that she might have meant that she wanted me to love her in that other sense, that larger sense, that sense beyond the physical senses.

So then, while we were in bed once, after we'd begun sleeping together occasionally, lying there this particular time in each other's arms after spending an hour or two pursuing the delights of the flesh, I began to think that I might love her, that I could love her, that perhaps I did love her, perhaps had loved her from the start—which was what I always thought about all the women I ever expended my energy in pursuing, senseless fascinations, hopeless hangings-of-the-heart upon patently unobtainable objects of affection or, perhaps more properly, lust or, even more accurately and darkly, some unnameable—or, at any rate, unnamed—passion, instinct, or perversion, all the more powerful for being compulsive, dangerous, obscure. Well, it wasn't so much that I thought I loved her as that I began to wonder if I did and I think it was the time I'm talking about that I began to imagine what it would be like to love her wholly and completely, not just physically, but emotionally and spiritually too, a way I had not thought of loving her before, mostly, I guess, because the chance of it seemed so remote, because I had so little encouragement from her to think that it might be possible, because...I don't know, I can't say, I don't remember exactly, but I do remember wondering at some time or other if perhaps I did love her, could love her, had loved her all along, and it was around that time I think that I remember at some point bumping into her at a party I hadn't thought she'd be at, a party that occurred some-time after we had begun going to bed together occasionally, her making it clear that this was not an exclusive thing, that she still had her long-time friends and one-time lovers and that I should too, because she wanted neither all her eggs in one basket nor to be the only egg in someone else's basket, which I thought was mixing things up a bit, but I got the point, so when I met her at this party I didn't have any expectations, although I certainly had my hopes, which I always had when she was around, or even when she wasn't around, even though I'd gone to the party thinking I'd probably meet some easy lay to wander home with, which I did in a way, in that I met her—an easy lay, it seemed, though not for me at that time, because I think this was before we started going to bed or maybe not, I can't really remember, but I know I met her at this party and had no expectations, was just being relaxed and loose and not feeling insecure when she fell into conversation with other, more attractive men, not wondering whether she had been to bed with this or that muscular hunk just the night before or was planning to be later that night, not standing there paralyzed by passion, able to think only of the fulfillment of my desire, the absolute indulgence of my lust, the pure and simple physical union whose realization was the constant content of my daily thoughts and nightly imaginings, masturbating continually in her honour, imagining her to be whoever I went to bed with, seizing hungrily on the least sign of interest from her, enlarging the dimensions of her smallest attention to the scale of my yearning, so that a smile at a joke I made became an indication of contented happiness in an ongoing life together, an agreement with my view on some matter of emotional dynamics or moral principle became a cornerstone of rapport upon which a lasting union would be built, a full-mouthed kiss became the basis of assurance for a perpetually satisfying sex life—not that I overloaded the situation: I wasn't the type to do that, being completely at ease in her presence now, and, learning that her car was in for repairs, offering her a ride home, an offer made without ulterior motive or disproportionate expectations, although I will admit to a slight tingle of anticipatory arousal when she smiled and nodded and squeezed my hand, saying, "Thanks, that'd be great." It was a little later, when the party was winding down, that I thought to be moving along and looked around and didn't see her, couldn't find her, felt a stab of panic knot my stomach, lost the thread of conversation I was in, excused myself to go downstairs to where the party was progressing on another level, didn't see her, couldn't find her, felt the stab of panic grow to desperation, returned upstairs to ask someone, "Have you seen Blackie?" trying to appear calm but, hearing they hadn't, being hardly able to contain my agitation, ascending to the floor above, where the party was progressing on still another level, didn't see her, couldn't find her, asked, descended two levels, asked, ascended another, and saw her standing by the kitchen table, sipping a drink and chatting with someone, smiling when I approached with utter calm, my panic dissipating the second I saw her, which was when I think I thought I loved her, no longer just wondering if I did, but really thinking I did, believing I did, but not saying I did, not even later, after the party, after I'd taken her home and we lay in bed beside each other that first time, if that was the first time, although I don't think it was, or perhaps a later time—yes, certainly a later time, oh months later, I'm sure, because I wore a worried expression, which I would not have worn that first time, fulfilling at last my fondest desire, achieving what I had hoped for, longed for, fantasized about for so many months, and finding, if I was to be totally honest, that it fell a little short of expectation, though not enough to cause me to wear a worried expression, which is what I wore a later time, oh months later, after we had gotten used to each other in bed and the minor dissatisfaction of that first time had evaporated along with the nervousness and tentativeness that had given rise to it and I wore a worried expression one night and she remarked on it, asking what was bothering me, which I couldn't tell her, because it wasn't clear to me: there seemed no reason to be worried, lying there with her in my arms, having just attained new heights in our lovemaking, fulfilling at last my fondest desire, achieving what I had hoped for, longed for, fantasized about for so many months, and wearing a worried expression, unable to say why, surprised by her asking, "Are you afraid to love me?" replying, "Perhaps," wondering if that was it, that I was afraid to love her, though I had thought I did, I think—love her, I mean: not feel afraid to love her, which I didn't think I felt, didn't consider I might feel, until she asked me if that was what I felt, although I may have been afraid to love her without feeling that I was afraid to love her, not that I even thought about it until she asked, thinking, as I think I've said, that I loved her, until, that is, she asked me if I was afraid to and I began to wonder if I was, and doubted that I did. Which I did. Doubt, I mean. Because I had thought I loved her, but now (or, rather, then) began to doubt that I did and wondered if I was afraid to. "Don't give it a thought," she said, kissing me, "I won't hurt you," kissing me, "It's better to love than not," kissing me, falling asleep beside me while I lay there, wearing a worried expression I couldn't explain.

10

Things were getting out of hand. Because Blackie's working schedule allowed us—on the occasions when we'd get together during the week—only the morning hours between about two (when she was available after finishing up at whatever club she was in) and eight or so (when I had to get up to go into the office), my work was suffering, I think, or at least I was told so by my boss, not that she knew enough to put it that way—I mean, she didn't say, "Look, your work is suffering; you've got to stop staying up till all hours of the night," because, of course, she didn't know that's what I was doing, but she did remark occasionally on my long lunches, during which (although she had no idea of this) I was driving to parks or malls and sleeping in the car in order to be able to face the rest of the day without snoring at my desk or drowsing off in a meeting, also so that I was fortified to endure her complaints about sales being down, expenses off target, corrective measures inadequate, records in disarray, forms improperly completed, prospects unpursued, tardiness habitual, profanity

unchecked, staff undisciplined, memos unanswered, account-
ants offended, clerks feeling terrorized, procedures ignored,
customers neglected, suppliers uncontrolled, appointments
missed, grammar inaccurate, manners forgotten, grooming
careless, attire inappropriate: I was a recalcitrant manager,
employee, person, being—unresponsive to criticism, falling
short of expectations and possibly (although this was never
said directly) in danger of being fired, a prospect more appealing than frightening, although it was that, I admit, since I really did need the income in order to maintain my standard of
living and I couldn't conceive of working up the enthusiasm
necessary to secure a new job while my energy was so
wrapped up in Blackie, who was with me now on more and
more occasions, sometimes as many as three times a week and
often throughout a weekend, although the weekends, by dint
of her having to work Saturday nights, were cruelly short...as,
in fact, were the weeknights, when, if we had arranged to get
together—and sometimes even if we hadn't—she would come
over to my place and wake me, share two or three hours of my
company and my bed, then go home to sleep or, as sometimes
happened, fall asleep in my bed, where I'd leave her a little
later, after I'd slumbered another hour or two before rising to
make my bleary-eyed entry at the office, where, as I say, my
stock was plummeting and I knew I should be spending more
time, but it was easier to call in sick than to crawl in
fatigued...not that I was derelict: I got the job done well
enough, whatever dissatisfactions they may have had with me
in various matters incidental to my main duties, none of
which latter I let slide too seriously, often working late into
the night before maybe leaving to meet Blackie and stay over

at her place, where we would indulge our prodigious sexual appetites amid the luxurious sensuality of her perfumed and dimly lit boudoir, the bedclothes adorned with feminine ruffles and frills, an environment from which I would regretfully depart just in time to be late again at work and struggle through another day of invoices and receipts, meetings and plans, sour looks and suspicious glances, after which I might drag myself home to sleep without eating, waking in the small hours, unable to resume my slumber—maybe it was too hot or too cold, or perhaps I was just restless, a condition I've always been prone to—and so I might venture forth into the dark streets to drive or walk for a time, until drowsiness drew me home or the dawn found me still wakeful and I would arrive uncharacteristically early at the office, prompting stupid jokes from fellow workers about whether I might not be ill or perhaps confused about the time of day. Anyway, it was such a night, I think—or perhaps I should say morning—that I found myself strolling around Blackie's neighbourhood, quite by chance, and somehow taking a notion to wander down the lane that ran back of her place, glancing up now and again past the various garages and fences at the darkened buildings and noticing a light on in her bedroom window, at which I felt a stab of...well, of something: I don't know—excitement, fear, arousal, curiosity, something of all of those, perhaps, but something anyhow that momentarily set my pulse running faster and my stomach churning, something which was, I know, physiologically speaking, adrenalin, but which sprang from I know not what precise emotional response to the yellow rectangle that, as I stood observing it, caused me to consider easing open the gate—which would creak noisily, I knew, but which I thought I might be able to edge back silently enough or at least quietly enough so as not to create too undue a sound until I could get through—and slipping across the lawn to position a crate where I could use it to get onto the roof of the shed under her window, which I knew was an absolutely crazy notion that I'd never have entertained had there been no light there, for I had no desire to intrude on her privacy, not being a peeping Tom. But the fact is that the light was there and it could mean either that she was out and had left it on unintentionally (learning which, I could just go on my way) or that she was in and might welcome an unexpected visit from me (which prospect I could pursue by going round to the front and ringing or knocking for admission, or maybe going to the nearest phone booth and calling beforehand to see if it was convenient) and the notion that had occurred to me would settle matters one way or the other, for from atop the shed I could see discreetly into the room, tell that it was empty or perhaps see her enter in a little white chemise with a lace trim at bodice and bottom, the seat of it snug in the crotch and cut high up her plush buttocks, her legs bare, her feet in high-heeled slippers that had little white puffballs on their single straps, the chemise pulling further into the crease of her trim little ass as she leaned towards the mirror of her vanity, where she spent an eternity fussing with her hair, brushing it out and tying it one way with a white ribbon, another way with a black, yet another way with two blue or pink ones, testing the effect of each from various angles, all of which I could observe from my vantage point on the shed's roof, crouching beneath the window and peering over the ledge to view her preening before a full-length three-panelled mirror, trying on a new dress, I guess, a slinky red number with black frills at bodice and hem, which she examined now from this side, now from that, stepping back a distance from the mirror and moving in close, running her hands up and down her sides against the smooth, tight-fitting fabric, looking over her shoulder to check the effect as she pushed out her buttocks, glancing sideways at the way it accentuated her breasts when she pulled back her shoulders and thrust out her bosom, spreading the slit of the skirt with two fingers at her right thigh and smiling a little mischievous smile at the length of black-stockinged leg thus revealed, while my heart raced and my chest constricted with short breaths I hardly dared breathe, whether for fear of the sound of them or out of sheer suspended anticipation, I couldn't say, only able to say in my mind: Take the fucking dress off, for Christ's sake! which she mercifully did after what seemed like an hour but was probably only five minutes or so, not that I could tell, since I was lost to time or time was lost to me, watching the zipper slide down the back of her dress, revealing soft, tanned flesh, with the black strap of her bra stretched across the alluring protuberance of her scapulas, which jutted out as she reached behind to undo the zipper to its end and the dress slid down to the floor, leaving her attired in bra and panties, garter belt and stockings, wearing which she walked over to her vanity and, leaning over so that the flimsy black fabric of her panties pulled tight into the crease between her buttocks, spent an eternity there before the mirror, tissuing off lipstick and removing makeup, fussing with her hair, brushing it out and tying it one way with a white ribbon, another way with a black, yet another way with two blue or pink ones, testing the effect of each from various angles, all of which I could observe from my vantage point on the shed's roof, crouching beneath the window to peer over the ledge, staring at the shapeliness of her legs, the beauty of her features intent on their image in the mirror, the roundness of her buttocks, the swells of her breasts barely contained by her bra, unaware that she was outside my window as I entered my bedroom, loosening my tie and sitting on the edge of the bed to unlace my shoes, pushing them off with the toe of one at the heel of the other, then stockinged toe at the heel of the first, lying back for a moment's rest and a brief reflection on the day's fatiguing events, rousing myself to remove my suit coat, moving to the closet to suspend the jacket on a hanger, pausing to rub the weariness out of my eyes, tugging at my tie and slowly undoing it, pulling it through my collar and hanging it on my tie rack, then observing myself in my full-length mirror, running my hands down from my chest and over the relative trimness of my belly, thumbs hooked briefly in the top of my pants as I rolled my head to relax the muscles of my neck and extended my arms, bending them up at the elbows to flex my biceps, initiating a long and luxurious stretch, twisting my torso, rotating my pelvis, tightening my legs, bending and swaying back and forth before straightening to begin languorously undoing my shirt buttons, after which I moved to the dresser, shirt undone but not removed, to divest myself of ring and wristwatch and to toy pensively with the hairs that curled on my chest and belly, hands slipping inside my pants and briefs to scratch lazily at my nuts, standing before the window, oblivious of her presence outside, her eager eyes following my every move, a small smile curving her lips at the sight of my private

male ritual, waiting with patient anticipation for the removal
of my clothes, a process that begins to take place, it seems, at
the very moment that she wishes it to, as though I were operating not out of my own volition but somehow at her command, obeying unconsciously the instructions she issues without utterance, shirttails pulled from constraints of pants, buckle undone, belt pulled out, pants unclasped, fly zipped down,
trousers dropped to the floor, stepped out of, hung up, a little
tour of the room in briefs and stockinged feet before sinking
down on the bed before the window, with legs outstretched to
reach down and remove my socks, after which I glance sideways at my image in the mirror, at the bulge in my bikini
briefs that enlarges in accompaniment to the accelerating
heartbeat, the weakness in arms and legs with which I respond
to her straightening up from her vanity and reaching behind
to unclasp her bra, shrugging the straps down over her shoulders and bending over again, allowing the garment to slide
down her arms, freeing pendulous breasts to my welcoming
view, my hands cupping my genitals for a brief indulgence of
autoeroticism that I view over my shoulder in the mirror by
my bed, trying to be impressed by the thrust I observe there,
ignorant of other eyes likewise engaged, the pane that frames
a scene for the watcher outside forming a mirror for the
watched inside, whose hands reach down to the strap of elas-
tic at the top of the underpants, lowering them over the rise
of the buttocks, down the thighs, the calves, the ankles, feet
stepping out of them, body lowered onto the bed for a brief
respite from the process of undressing, an exultant liberation
from the strictures of clothing, the hands straying over the
body, lingering at nipple, at thigh and buttock, settling finally

in the genital area, to stroke and pull there, probe and flutter, fondle and press, legs pulled up and bent at the knee, thighs bristling with a mat of hair, thighs sleek in their nylon stockings, hand pumping furiously, fingers plunging piston-like, watchers breathless, nerves tingling, pulses racing, stomachs churning, limbs weakened, eyes burning, bodies freezing with agonizing clutches of panic in the beams of light and the harsh shout: "Police!...Don't move!"—blood draining down to legs weakened still more, asshole tightening against a fluid drop in the bowels, tiny pinpoints of light circling dizzyingly, dizzily, in peripheral vision, a self-perceived halo of brilliant yellow, a maroon aura somehow beheld by eyes that stare fixedly, fingers scraping on brick for a hold to sustain the body that sags and would sink to the dew-damp lawn outside my window, sliding down the sharp incline of the shed roof I wish I'd never climbed, a rough hand clutching the soft, numbed shoulder, an imperious voice announcing, "I'm placing you under arrest, ma'am," which I hear through the crack that my window is opened, feeling a brief anesthesia of terror that quickly gives way to a trembling and turbulence, hand first frozen on, swiftly left hold of my tumescent member that shrivels and shrinks at the voice saying, "Come with me—just over here," and here is a place where a second cop has his gun trained on me, causing my knees to give out as the zipper slides down to reveal her soft white back with the black strap of her bra stretched across the alluring protuberance of her scapulas, which jut out as she reaches behind to undo the zipper to its end and the dress slides down to the floor, leaving her attired in bra and panties, garter belt and stockings, wearing which she walks over to her vanity and, leaning over so that the flimsy black fabric of her panties pulls tight into the crease between her buttocks, spends an eternity there, while I'm told to turn facing the shed beneath her window, my arms stretched above me against the wall, his hands running down from my chest over the relative trimness of my belly, along my sides and over my hips, round the taut muscles of my buttocks, down my legs, then grasping my arm, saying, "Just come with me to the cruiser, please, ma'am," and asking her for identification, which I don't have on me, my name given, written down, a knock on her door that she responds to with perturbation, trepidation, puzzlement, wondering what's going on, hearing the officer give me my name, asking if this is a person known to me and explaining that if I have colour of right to the property I am not under arrest and she's free to go and I tell them of course, she's my girlfriend, it was all a misunderstanding, I don't understand what's going on here, my bathrobe hastily thrown on and clutched about me, being told, "Okay, she says you're a friend of hers. You're no longer under arrest," and, in response to my query, "No, you won't have a record," telling her, "Try to see that this doesn't happen again ma'am. You could be charged with prowl-by-night, except he vouched for you," and her collapsing into my arms after they'd gone, sobbing hard enough to break my heart, saying, "If you'd keep your blinds closed this wouldn't have happened," saying, "I know, Blackie, I know...I'm sorry, I'm sorry...I don't know what got into me...you looked so beautiful...I'm sorry to cause you all this trouble and fright...I'm sorry...I'll never do it again...Oh hold me, hold me, please, I'm sorry." "You asshole! What a dumb thing to do! I should have told them I never heard of you!" "Blackie, I'm sorry..." and on and on for I don't know how long, being lost to time or time lost to me, adrift on the cloud of her multiple fragrances, cushioned on her bosom, consoled by her kisses, comforted by her embrace, aroused by her caresses, stirred by her tears, moved by the passion with which she made, with which we made love lost to time lost to us.

11

There was a party that Blackie had said she might be at and that I had said I'd probably have to miss, a post-opening celebration of someone's first solo exhibition at an important gallery, the date and time coinciding with the flight arrival of a visiting executive who my boss insisted should be met at the airport by me, the manager who (according to her) would benefit most from the visit, and who had, if truth be told, begged off too many of these assignments in the past to fairly get away with it again for a while, all of which meant that I wound up extending social and chauffeurial courtesies to a semi-alcoholic bore whose company I was unable to escape until well into the evening, thus missing the public exhibit entirely and arriving at the private party when it was in full swing, wondering if I'd missed Blackie—which I hadn't, since she was there; but which I may as well have, since we wound up circulating separately for most of what was left of the evening and...well, I don't remember exactly how it came about, but we happened to be leaving at the same time and I

offered her a ride home, to which she replied that she had her
car, thanks very much, so I suggested that she might drop by
my place on her way and she said maybe she would and smiled
then and said "Okay" to a man who was putting on his coat
or who maybe was not putting on his coat but simply leaving,
because I can't remember (or maybe don't want to) whether
it was the time of year that would require a coat or the time
of year that wouldn't, not that the time of year matters at all,
except that these things bother me (the time of year when
things happen, I mean), so I always try to determine to the best
of my ability exactly when it was that things happened,
whether it was fall or spring or winter or summer, which I
think it was, one of those, as he smiled and made a little circle
with his thumb and index finger and put his coat on and left
or just left without putting on his coat because he didn't have
one, the weather not requiring it, her saying to me, "See ya
'round," and leaving, leaving me to look around at a bunch of
people I maybe knew or maybe didn't know, but didn't want
to be with, finishing my drink and maybe another one before
leaving and driving past her place an hour or two later to see
the fluorescent black light on in her bedroom at the front of
the second floor, a light she always only used when she was
making love, as she had so often with me, turning on the light
that picked up all the white of her fluffy duvet and frilled pil-
low slips and silk sheets, saying, "Makes it nicer, doesn't it?
More romantic...sexxxier," drawing out that sibilance in the
middle of the word "sexier," welcoming me into her arms,
wriggling down with her head between my legs and arranging herself with my head between hers, everything rearranged
again later, when we were both ready, her with her legs lifted

and bent at the knees, in a kind of fetal position that allowed me to enter her, soon after which she splayed her legs, grasping her feet with her hands and rocking back and forth, moaning and panting and whispering words of endearment to him as he thrusts deeper and deeper within her, feeling his balls against her buttocks, her hands fluttering over his scrotal hairs, creating little electric thrills that intensify his excitement, inspire him to stronger and deeper thrusts that elicit from her a rippling sequence of sharp little intakes of breath, as I idle the motor in the darkened street, then circle the block again to be sure I have not just imagined the whole thing: the two cars outside her house with motors cooling, ticking still, as I stand near them, knowing hers, figuring the other his, sensing the extra heat from them both in the already hot summer street, I think; or rather, feeling the heat of them in the subzero weather, although whether that is accurate or not I couldn't say, can't say, can only say, I think, that I left the party within minutes of their separate departures to amble nonchalantly down the street and around the corner to where my car was parked, casually settling myself and warming the motor for the journey home, with no intention of waiting an extra few minutes to give them a head start before taking a route to my place that would lead me past her place, where I saw the two cars in the street and parked and slipped out and walked past the cars, hearing the contracting metal of their motors ticking in the silent street and checking the licence on hers to be sure it was hers and not just an identical make and model and year, then walking around the block, returning to see the lights in the front of the house turned off, then slipping round the side to the back, where her bedroom was, on the ground floor, the curtains lit with the little blue incandescent light that she always turned on only when she was making love, saying, "Mmmmm...there, that's better, eh?" after turning off the overhead light and snuggling in beside me in the blue glow, in the big brass bed with the powder-blue comforter and pale-blue pillowcases, pulling the blue flannel sheets up around us with their welcome warmth in the winter night as she turns to him with a gentle smile and begins to play with the hairs on his chest, rubbing her legs against his, kissing him on the mouth at first lightly, teasingly, then deeply, fixedly, tongues probing in mutual exploration, the rustlings and sighings and moanings and pantings carried on the heavy summer night air through the window opened wide to catch any slight breeze that might rise, as I slink stealthily away to linger at the party, having held her in conversation as long as I could, the man she'd said "Okay" to having gone, with or without his coat, she herself clearly about to go, not really paying attention to the things I keep finding to say to her, the story I stretch out to keep her from leaving, which she finally does, breaking into my story to say she really has to go and she'll hear the rest of it another time, which she probably won't, because I'll never remember, not really interested in telling it, as such, but merely in keeping her from leaving as long as I can because I know she's going with that lean, tanned, muscular son of a bitch, leaving me to linger at the party, sullenly sipping a warming drink, with no heart for conversation, no capacity for being with others, her the only other I want to be with, the two of us alone in the little third-floor bedroom, where dim light glowed from the two small candles she always only lit when she was making love, saying, "It's lilac...like it?" as the blended fragrances of her candles and her perfume mingle in my nostrils, as the light plays off stray wisps of her hair to create a small gold halo, flickers gold on her naked body, lends a rich bronze lustre to her swaying breasts that I rise to meet as she bends down to him with a gentle smile, and I press my face to her bosom with a sigh, hearing the answering sigh that she breathes in his ear, her head sunk down to kiss, with infinite tenderness, the spiralling chamber she begins softly to lick, gradually closing her mouth upon it, swirling her tongue with increasing intensity, the warm gusts of her breath setting off a sequence of exquisite little explosions that ripple along his nerves, into his neck and down his spine, the sensations so intense that his back contracts in a spasm of excruciating pleasure and his cock swells and bobs against her thigh, as I tug with my teeth at her stiffening nipples, first one, then the other, my hands caressing the plush cushions of her buttocks, fingers slipping into the crevice between, down and along to the warm, moist orifice, feeling her fingers fluttering gently along the length of his cock, arching herself back so that my mouth moves down from her breasts and over her belly, down to the dark tuft of hair and the soft lips of her cunt, her hands running over his body as she repositions herself and licks lightly at his cock, then takes it into her mouth, feeling the bulging veins and the wrinkled flesh, the swollen head rubbing against the roof of her mouth, as I stay hard while she rides my cock to the height of her pleasure, reaching back now and again to feather her hands along his balls, the chill air of the winter night making me shiver as I stood in the street under the window where the candlelight flickered, becoming aware that I'd left my overcoat in the car or at the party, most likely at the party, which I decided to return to, trembling with cold in the humid summer night, glancing continually back at the pale fluorescent light from her first-floor bedroom, covering several blocks of snow-encrusted streets before I realized my car was back near her place, where the blue light shone from the second-floor window, and so hailed a taxi I took to the party to retrieve my coat, throngs of people still there, overflowing onto the porch and sidewalk in the balmy spring weather, no one noticing my return, a handful of folk remaining, donning windbreakers and trench coats against the brisk autumn breezes, looking at me quizzically as I searched for a coat that wasn't there, then stopped to talk a moment with Blackie, exchanging pleasantries and saying I wouldn't keep her, noticing that she was smiling at a man who seemed to be looking for something—his coat, perhaps, although I can't remember whether it was weather that required one, but I noticed he made a little circle with the thumb and forefinger of his right hand just after she laughed and said "Okay" and I told her I'd hear her story later, I really had to be going, I had a taxi waiting, no, I didn't need a coat against the winter cold, I had one back in my car, it was nice to see her again, we'd have that dinner I'd promised her, maybe in an outdoor café now the weather was nice and she was taking a week off from work, but I really had to go now, glancing past her, catching the eye of the lean, tanned, full-figured woman who smiled at me as she put on her coat or maybe didn't put on her coat but just smiled and blew me a kiss as I raised my hand and made a little circle with my thumb and forefinger, saying "Okay," and looked around and didn't see her, couldn't find her, felt a stab of panic knot my stomach, lost the thread of conversation I was in, excused myself to go downstairs to where the party was progressing on another level, didn't see her, couldn't find her, felt the stab of panic grow to desperation, returned upstairs to ask someone, "Have you seen Blackie?" trying to appear calm but, hearing they hadn't, hardly able to contain my agitation, ascending to the floor above, where the party was progressing on still another level, didn't see her, couldn't find her, asked, descended two levels, asked, ascended another, and saw her standing by the kitchen table, sipping a drink and chatting with someone, smiling and saying "Okay" with utter calm, my panic intensifying the second I saw her, which was when I think I thought I loved her, no longer just wondering if I did, but really thinking I did, believing I did, but not saying I did, not even later, oh months later, after the party, after I'd taken her home and we lay in bed beside each other that first time, if that was the first time, although I would not have worn a worried expression that first time, fulfilling at last my fondest desire, achieving what I had hoped for, longed for, fantasized about for so many months, and finding, if I was to be totally honest, that it exceeded my expectations, though I wore, she told me, a worried expression, which I can't believe I would have worn that first time, not that she'd lie, god forbid, not her, she wouldn't do that, certainly not her, not the type to lie, not like me, who might lie at a moment's notice, unintentionally of course, I wouldn't mean to lie, don't want to lie, but may lie, as I did lie, oh months later, after we had gotten used to each other, lying in bed with her when she remarked on the worried expression I wore, surprising me by asking, "Are you afraid to love me?"—to which I lied, I mean replied, "Perhaps," knowing she was right, that I was afraid to love her. "Don't give it a

thought," she said, kissing me, "I won't hurt you," kissing me,
"It's better to love than not," kissing me, falling asleep beside
me while I lay there, wearing a worried expression, trembling
with cold in the winter air or the humid summer night, but in
any case trembling, watching the blue fluorescent light of the
two incandescent black candles that she always only lit when
she was making love, afloat on billowing clouds of pillows and
comforter, waterbed mattress and downy cushions, silk sheets
and flannel coverlet, brass bed and unfolded futon, mirrored
walls and mirrored ceiling that reflected her fucking him, up
on the third floor, down on the first, round through the second, the shouts and screams of their unbridled passion echo-
ing over the quiet dawn streets I wandered for hours, unable
to sleep, wondering, What will her neighbours think? Who'll
call the cops? that is, What if her neighbours should call the
police, mistaking the screaming and hollering as signals of rape
or murder or worse? as their howls and bellows and shrieks
and squeals reverberate off the silent bricks of the sleeping city
I drive my car through, windows down to take advantage of
the brief respite of cooling dawn, or up to guard against the
vicious bite of another winter day, stopping at some early-
opened market for groceries I don't want and don't need, just
seeking diversion, anything to avoid returning home to the
loneliness and silence, wandering the aisles of the store, hearing my name spoken, turning to face some acquaintance
who's up early or out late but in either case is in a talkative
mood, asking me this, telling me that, raving about a theatre
performance he'd been to the night before that had showcased
the talents of some famous Irish actress, the evening concluding with a staging of the Molly Bloom soliloquy, the set for

which he rhapsodized over at length, describing the large brass bed and the fluffy white coverlet, the big white pillows, the lacy nightgown, remarking how richly feminine it all was and looking puzzled when I quickly concluded the conversation and turned away so he wouldn't see, welling in my eyes, the tears that flowed freely once I regained the privacy of my car and drove home to the loneliness and silence, where I found myself thinking of the party at which she'd accepted my offer of a ride, the panic I'd felt when I couldn't find her, the thought I had had that I loved her, the panic erupting anew now, not just a memory, spiralling up from the pit of my stomach, so sharp and hot and unrelenting that I sank to the floor with a groan, stretching against the searing sensation, crawling around on my hands and knees, tears streaming, face contorted, guts twisting, knees dragged burning across the rug, fists aching from pounding the floor, the desperation clawing inside me, a strand of barbed wire raked up to rip at my chest, a river of lava that bursts from my mouth in a crescendo wail, a living thing, it seemed, that I realized then had been eating me up and I stared in horror, sobbing and screaming, "That's not love! That's not *love*! Oh Jesus, fuck, Christ almighty! Fucking Jesus! Son of a bitch! That's not love! Oh *what*? Oh fuck! Oh Jesus Christ! Oh that's not love!" until I lay exhausted, the violent emotion subsiding, and mumbled repeatedly through my lessening tears, "That's not love, that's not love," knowing it wasn't, not knowing what was, nor what it was I'd just felt, nor what it was I had felt all along that I'd thought might be love, but instead was perhaps just affection or lust or passion or perversion or maybe simple attraction, or possibly even a mix of them all, but in any case wasn't love, except insofar as those elements may be components of love, which they may be, I don't know, I can't say, I only know that I knew then that I wasn't in love with her, hadn't been in love with her, knowing nothing beyond that, nothing at all except a feeling of emptiness, of wanting something but not knowing what, only that it wasn't that, not that coiling, searing, consuming something I'd felt, which I thought might be jealousy, but which, if it was, had been there before I met her. For I thought, as I lay there, of the night I first saw her and the burning urgency that had drawn me to the club before I knew she was there, that had increased when I'd seen her, had persisted and ruled me, as it had so often with so many others, and that seemed now like a junior version of what I'd just experienced, as though what now was acute and intensely focused had been there always, but eating more slowly, less hungrily, chronically, as though all my former obsessions with women were all wrapped up in Blackie, which they may have been, I didn't know, I couldn't say, could only say, sotto voce, over and over, "That's not love," weeping diminuendo, perhaps for the loss of imagined love, or for some other, older loss or absence, I don't know, I can't say.

I slept.

12

At first, only darkness and slight sounds: a heartbeat, breathing, slosh of liquid through pipe or gutter; and the sense of being cramped and constricted in a room built to the scale of much smaller beings. A sudden glare of light, generalized, soon resolved into a brief white rectangle that is quickly filled with flickering images, the objects in the room mantled with a dull glow, brighter rays emanating somewhere back and to the side of me from a bulb within a metal housing, the continuous sound of sloshing liquid modulating to the whir of a small fan cooling an electric motor, the breathing become the hum of the motor itself, the heartbeat the rhythmic clicks of the sprockets as the film rolls off the reel, projecting a black-and-white image, shot with unsteady hand, of the house of my childhood, which is the house in which I sit watching a home movie that shows me crawling out the front door, a pudgy baby in floppy-brimmed bonnet and fluffy jumper; a smile, a drool, a squint, and a tumble, at which I hear my father's laughter, as he leans forward in the dim light reflected from the screen to flick ashes from his cigarette, his face a study in mirth, his presence a mystery to me for a reason I can't at first specify, but which gradually becomes clear: he shouldn't be here, because he died several years ago, and though I long to lean towards him and ask, "Didn't you die? How'd you get back?" some innate sense informs me that it would not be polite to do so, and besides, I seem to recall asking something like that on a previous occasion when he'd turned up somewhere unexpectedly and he just ignored the question, looking at me briefly and winking, then making a joke about the racetrack and laughing, smiling and nodding at me as though there was something unspoken but well understood between us, which nonetheless remains unclear to me, and I am about to remove myself to the kitchen to ask of my mother, who is cooking supper or preparing a pie for baking, how come Dad is here after having died years ago, when I realize that it would be pointless to do so, since she herself died not long after him and would be no more prepared than he to respond to my query. I arise nevertheless and enter the kitchen, which is vast and sombre, dimly illuminated beneath vaulting arches by large torches set in iron fittings on the two rows of pillars that run down either side of the expansive nave, the flames picking up dark reds and blues in stained-glass windows depicting biblical scenes and haloed saints, a procession of hooded, candle-bearing figures shuffling down the long centre aisle, white robes reaching to the flagstone floor, a devotional murmur accompanying their progress, the slow, solemn drone of organ notes vibrating dully on the air. At the front of the nave, before the main altar, there stands a low, marble-topped railing at which we all kneel, and from my place in the row of worshippers I examine a stained-glass window behind the altar, discovering that it depicts not a biblical but an erotic scene, as do, I now notice, all of the windows in the cathedral: here a scene of fellatio, there of cunnilingus, another of anal intercourse, others of coitus in various positions, all of the participants attired in the loose robes of antiquity. Wondering how I had failed to realize this before, I see that the window to my right has, in its lower left-hand corner, a representation of Mickey Mouse toiling away at a sweating, writhing Daisy Duck, with a thought balloon hovering above them both, connected to each by a string of bubbles and containing the words "Hope Donald doesn't come home!" I begin to turn to my neighbour, intending to point out that the thought balloon is poorly considered, since Donald and Daisy never lived together, when the music and voices cease and a figure at the altar proceeds solemnly down the steps and approaches the railing, standing before me in a purple cloak with a gold trim around the neck and hem and down both sides where it joins at the front. The face is in shadow. The air is heavy with the odour of incense. The figure speaks with the voice of Black Satin, arms lifting within the cloak to part it at the front to reveal her nakedness, and saying, "This is my body; take and eat of it," at which I am struck with fear and hear a voice beside me say, "Abandon all hope, ye who enter here," whereupon the director interrupts and castigates me for wearing an inappropriate expression, concluding by demanding my union card, which I know I don't have but begin to search about my person for, only to discover that I am naked. The director orders me to leave, and as I reach the cathedral's main door, Blackie appears beside me, saying, "I'm going too. This is a stupid movie." I thought she was the producer, but not wanting to reveal my ignorance, make no mention of it. She is dressed now in jeans and a T-shirt, and I suddenly recall that I have some clothes stashed in the basement of the church, where I am eager to go to retrieve them, feeling desperately embarrassed at my nudity, but she insists that there's no time and we pass through the door to the accompaniment of joyfully tolling bells and a cheering, jolly crowd who shower us with rice and confetti, an endless line of men availing themselves of the opportunity to kiss the bride, who accepts far more than kisses: caresses, fondling, lifting of her T-shirt, undoing of her jeans, giving as good as she gets; while I circulate among friends, asking to borrow articles of clothing and being refused. Blackie and I finally enter a stretch limousine that is being driven by my boss, who stops at a confectionery store, Blackie having expressed a desire to pick up some candy. I remain in the car, not wanting to appear naked in public, and while we're waiting for Blackie, there are sounds of gunfire from further back down the street and people start running past us, some with red blotches of blood on their clothing. A man falls, apparently dead, across the hood of the car, at which my boss, who is not my boss but the lean, tanned, muscular man that Blackie left that party with, pulls away, ignoring my pleas to stop, to let me rescue Blackie from the carnage. We arrive at a deserted country road and he tells me this is my address, I must get out, which I do because I don't know what else to do. He drives away, leaving me lost and alone.

In a room I don't recognize, lost and alone, I strain to perceive unfamiliar objects taking dim shape in gray twilight of dawn or dusk, pale yellow glow of headlights from a passing car sending across the ceiling the window frame's shadow: stretched, condensed, and stretched again; the rush of wind and motor dying on the air of ambiguous time, as I make out a mirror, a desk, a chair, television, easy chair, table and lamp, foot of bed, spread and blanket and sheet that I lie under, struggling to form, through leaden weight in brain and body, some recollection of where I am and what I'm doing here, gradually aware that the furniture comprises the bland and anonymous essentials to be found in any hotel room, feeling no less lost and alone for the realization, nor for that of the city or town, nor the reason for my being there, nor the time of day or evening, nor anything else, for try as I might to pretend that I'm not, I'm lost and alone in unconditional loss and loneliness, regardless of hotel room or home, hobby or job, companion or friend. The loss and the loneliness stretch back past Blackie. I know that—lying there in the dim haze of the dying or beginning day, in whatever city or town I had travelled to for whatever reason, probably to lose myself (though I was already lost) in the details of travel, the effort of displacement, of contending with a different environment, hoping thereby to take my mind off the distress that beset it, to avoid the brooding I'd fallen prey to, not that I had any right to brood really, for she'd never deceived me, never betrayed me, only persisted in just what she said she would, even though she told me to love her, which I didn't do, however much I may have thought I had, thinking I was in love with her when I was actually lost in her, losing myself in her as I had lost myself in others before her, but never so badly, never so thoroughly, never so long, so lost to myself, which I must have been always without ever knowing it, knowing at last how lost and alone I am...was...had been...waking at an uncertain hour in an unknown city during an indeterminate season, not knowing where I am nor what I'm doing there, straining to perceive familiar objects that won't take shape in a room I don't recognize, gradually aware that the loss and the loneliness stretch back past Blackie, taking dim shape in the pale yellow lights of a passing car, a chair, a television, brain and body struggling to form, time ambiguous, room anonymous, shadows gray, lost and alone, regardless of Blackie, regardless of time, of home or hotel room, hobby or job, friend or companion, time lost to me lost to time lost to Blackie betraying me, Blackie deceiving me, Blackie persisting in just what she said she would, promising nothing and leaving me nothing to brood about everything gray indeterminate dusk or dawn of unformed time of nothing forming thought or feeling dull and disconsolate shadow on ceiling or bed or streets of a city or town whose name I forget remembering nothing I remember exactly the way I began to forget the way I'd begun to think I loved Blackie who only persisted in dull indeterminate brooding on everything I remember ambiguous something she said once to love her forgetting I guess that she'd said I remember nothing she said to me leaving me just as she found me forgetting I'd always been lost and alone in a city or town where I worshipped a woman forgetting me only who wanted to love who I wanted to love me forgetting myself I remember at first only nothing and wanting for any getting I ever got nothing ambiguous nothing of only persisting in just what I wanted for any worship is fearing she frightened me always alone and never lost never let out of her sight when she needed to hit me she hit me what Blackie had hit me with I couldn't handle wanting love couldn't handle wanting Blackie and not having her have any man she wanted any time she cared to having lovers having me having nothing and not wanting anything only darkness and slight sounds a car going by on the road outside the window makes nothing matter more than having her love me whoever she is preparing for baking a pie in the empty oven waiting warm in the huge kitchen I remember not mattering when she was baking a cake for baby and me in her arms after she snatched me out of the pile of knives I'd spilled a shadow on my arm or leg of blood she held me underneath the tap that made me melt and feel like nothing ever more than me I wanted something still and don't know what or why I feel like never have been more than anything that fits inside a room that has no light with knowing not the town or city nor the reason for my being there a chair or bed within a room wet sticky red liquid water glass of anonymous mirror image of no matter forming more than an image of matter spilling out of nothing no matter what am I of matter knowing only I deceived myself alone and lost beside myself in time betrayed by only me forgetting myself on a bed remembering where I lay doesn't matter what or who she is has nothing to do with her or her who all I have remembrance of is lying in a room full of unfamiliar objects leaden dawn or dusk of shadows in a glass or on a white rectangle of nothing I remember only gray indeterminate nothing

13

I returned to the city with a firm and committed plan to organize my life in a manner that would minimize the possibility of meeting her or thinking about her, determined to bury myself in my work and to avoid any place she might be or that might remind me of her, staying away from galleries and strip clubs, from the neighbourhood she lived in, after-hours clubs she went to, mutual friends and acquaintances and all the places they frequented, throwing myself into hobbies I'd long neglected and seeking out new ones, joining an equestrian club, a health club, a racquet club, a bridge club, taking up flying, cooking, cycling, jogging, baseball, hockey, attending movies, plays, poetry readings, art lectures—wait, no, not art lectures, never art lectures, God forbid I should wind up at an art lecture, not that she'd attend them but they fell into the category of things that would remind me of her, which I had to avoid at all costs, not that I could, of course, not that I did, not that I managed half the things I intended, most of which, upon closer examination, proved to have, at least in my mind, some kernel of association with her, plays putting me in the position of witnessing a performance on a stage, the riding crop reminding me of an act she used to do with a whip, cycling calling up images of the bikers who controlled most of the strip clubs, hockey entailing wearing a garter belt to hold up the hockey socks, and anyway, ordering my life on the basis of physical or mental avoidance meant that instead of trying to anticipate where she might be in order to see her I spent all my time doing the same thing in order not to see her, so I was still thinking about her, still structuring my life around her, comparing other women to her, going to a stag for someone at the office and wondering if she'd be the stripper they hired, walking into a bar and experiencing an electric tingle in my veins when I heard her name, which turned out not to be her name but a reference to a black satin garment someone had bought or was going to buy, sitting in a restaurant and hearing a voice that sounded like hers, seeing a woman with black hair ahead of me on the street or in a department store and thinking it was her, answering the phone at home, a few weeks after I got back, to hear her say, "Hi! Whatcha been doin'? Haven't seen you in weeks." The space my heart took up in my mouth barely left room for all the bullshit I came up with about being really busy with work and being out of town and having almost no chance to get out anywhere, all of which gave rise on her part to expressions of sympathy and the hope that I could squeeze out a bit of time for a drink, because she had the evening free, having taken a week off bookings to concentrate on her painting and she needed some company after working alone in the studio all day, so come on, why didn't I take a break from the work I'd brought home, but I had so much to do, it really wasn't a good idea, oh what a stick-in-the-mud, an hour or two wouldn't hurt and it would probably refresh me so I'd work all the better, except, look, if I didn't have this report (I didn't have any report to do) on the president's desk before nine, I could kiss my ass goodbye, well she knew a better ass for me to kiss or didn't I like her anymore, but I didn't want to see her, didn't want to have the hard-on I was getting, didn't want to tell her what I'd have to tell her when I saw her, sitting there so pretty and smiling, saying, "Now, isn't this pleasant? Aren't you glad I talked you into it?" while I faked a bit of a smile and started trying to find the words to say to her that—but she got right into talking about her painting and saying she wasn't going to be coy, she had a favour to ask me, a big favour since I was so busy, but she just had to have me sit for her because this painting she was doing, all built around eyes, had a space that just cried out to have my eyes in it and would I please, my eyes were the only ones that would do, and I could have cried my eyes out then but there was no space for that, I couldn't sit in a bar beside her crying my eyes out over the space between us, especially since it was a space that apparently she didn't feel and so I asked, without a trace of bitterness, why she didn't get the guy she left the party with to do it, her hand holding a lit match stopping halfway to her cigarette, then shaking out the match, placing it in the ashtray, removing the cigarette from her mouth, her smile dying, her eyebrows lifting, her voice asking, "Just what does that bitter little remark mean?" "It was not a remark," I informed her, "but a question." Eyes rolled briefly ceilingwards, then as briefly closed, then fixing on me, and, "Look, don't play any bullshit word games with me, okay?

If you've got a problem with the way I live my life, it's your problem and I don't need any trips laid on me." "No, you get laid enough." Oh, not a noble moment for me, and I deserved her silent glare, her calm placing on the table of the money for her drink, her quick and wordless departure, her leaving me to finish my drink in morose solitude, to linger and gradually rise above my smoldering anger, to regain my composure and turn on my charm for the little blonde who came in later and sat at the bar and left with me an hour or two after, except it wasn't going to be so easy, because instead of walking out on me with patient dignity, Blackie said simply, "You're above that kind of childish comment," and I felt the hot suffusion of a blush rise from my chest and redden my face as we sat in silence until I found the strength to apologize and the courage to tell her that I felt hurt that night when she left the party with him, that I knew she'd never promised me anything, though she did ask me to love her, that she had no obligation to me, though she did say she wouldn't hurt me, that we'd agreed this wasn't an exclusive thing between us, though I hadn't gone to bed with anyone else for months, that I wasn't trying to tie her down, though I couldn't bear to witness her affairs, that I knew she didn't love me, though...though...though I didn't know what and I did avert my eyes, looking off to one side and feeling her hand on mine or glancing down at my drink and seeing her hand on mine or raising my eyes to the mirrored ceiling and noticing the reflection of her hand on mine or bumping into someone I knew a couple days later who asked, "Who was that I saw you with in the bar the other night, sitting there with her hand on yours?" or seeing a picture in a magazine a few weeks later of some woman sitting in a bar with her hand on some guy's hand, and able to look her in the eye, I'm sure, although I don't remember whether I did or not because they were watering, my eyes, I mean, not that I was crying, but my eyes were watering, and I moved the ashtray a bit so the cigarette smoke wouldn't drift into my eyes, which were watering, so that I used the little napkin my drink was resting on to dry my eyes and repositioned the ashtray so the smoke wouldn't make my eyes water as she brushed her hand slowly over mine and said, "I'm sorry you were hurt, I really am. I didn't mean to hurt you. He was just very attractive and...well...I did have second thoughts when you asked me to go with you, but...Please don't ask me to explain, okay?...I didn't know you were this serious, or..." Or what, I wondered, never asking, never knowing, never saying all perhaps I could have said, all I maybe should have said: hadn't loved her, didn't want her, couldn't see her, wouldn't sit for any painting, wished her hand was not on mine, wished her voice was not conciliatory, couldn't stand her eyes' compassion, couldn't bear the things I felt, resolve weakening, desire strengthening, heart softening, cock hardening, eyes watering, hand gripping hers, voice choking, mouth moving, trying to say, "I think I love you," just because I thought I did, I mean I think I tried to say, "I thought I loved you," just because, I think, I thought I did, I mean I said, "I think I love you," or I thought I did or think I thought I did or thought, I think, I love you, thinking, I think, to move my lips around those words I think I thought, I love her, forming in my mind, a thought I think I thought or tried to form around her, tried to love her, tried to think, to form my lips around the thought I loved to think, to think I loved her, tried to say, "I love you," tried to form the words I thought I'd—"What are you think-ing?" she asked. "Oh...I don't know," I said, stroking her hand. "When do you want me to sit for you?"

14

The sitting was arranged for a Tuesday, which (as I said to her in my phone call on that day) I had forgotten was when we always held our weekly planning meeting at the office, an event that had to be kept open-ended and that sometimes went overtime—well, yes, it *was* the first time she'd heard of that, because it had never before been a factor in any of our plans, I hadn't wanted to bore her with *all* the details of my office routine, but anyway, this thing was a reality and it occasionally extended into the evening, as it was very likely to do this particular time, since there were some knotty problems to be worked out, and I wouldn't want to inconvenience her in the event that it did run late, having her waiting around for me to perhaps not be able to arrive at all or, at best, get there and have to leave before she managed to accomplish anything, so it only made sense to postpone the sitting, and as the rest of the week was already overcommitted, we'd better make it for the following Wednesday, when it was again necessary for me to phone with my apologies, this time for having taken sick, but surely I'd be recovered by the weekend and we could do it then, only (as I explained in another call) a pipe broke the Friday night and the plumber never got there till late Saturday and I had to be around on Sunday because the job stretched out, getting more complicated (as these things often will) the more the matter progressed, so that we planned for the following Thursday, after her work at one of the clubs, except that halfway to her place I had to call from a phone booth with the news that my car had broken down and I'd have to get it towed to my mechanic's garage, by which time the evening would be shot, but yes: the weekend—wait, no, I'd promised to help some friends set up their new apartment, painting and that kind of thing, and they were really depending on me…Yes, of course, I wanted "to do this thing," as she put it; it wasn't my fault all these obstacles kept throwing themselves up in my path, and both our schedules were hectic, I was doing my best, no, I wasn't avoiding her, yes, I would make a firm commitment for the subsequent Monday, no, better make it Tuesday, oh, but there was that weekly meeting again, so Wedn—uh, wait, heavy day on Thursday, I'd have to be alert, okay, two weekends hence, on the Sunday, her day off, a free day for me, yes, I knew that made it a full month or more since I'd first promised and, believe me, nothing short of a death in the family or my own death would keep me from it, but no, she shouldn't have me stay for dinner, I wouldn't have her cooking, she should concentrate on her painting, I'd treat her to a restaurant meal, but…well, if she really insisted on preparing something in advance that could just be left to heat in the oven while she worked, why that would be wonderful, not necessary, really, but thank you, sure, more than just a token of her appreciation, too generous, really, and please, let me contribute the wine, yes, it would certainly be fun, I was looking forward to it immensely...God knows, I always enjoy spending hours stifling my feelings, putting on a false front, hiding my misery, holding back tears, wishing she wouldn't make those beguiling little gestures—a tug with her teeth at her lower lip, a tilt of her head to left or right—that I can see in my peripheral vision every now and again when she stops to deliberate for a second before trying another pen-and-ink study of my eyes, which she has me hold on a fixed point off to the side, chastising me gently now and again for not holding the pose, there was something to be said for professional models, could I just keep my eyes on that spot above the window, from which they kept straying to feast for a second or two on the turn of her ankle just above her sneaker—she *would* have to wear sneakers without socks—or the drop of her smock to the tight thigh of her paint-spattered jeans, or the wisp of hair at her temple, and why is there not a law that artists must wear bras when having their subjects pose, as I strain to fulfill my obligation to stare where I'd rather not stare and avert my eyes from where I long to let them linger, having found no way to avoid this appointment, no war having broken out in my neighbourhood, no act of God or natural disaster to prevent my attendance, no death in the family or death of me, which this endurance test would surely be, the long afternoon hours measured by honey-coloured rays of sun creeping across the studio floor and up the wall, glinting off her wineglass, lightening the deep red of the Beaujolais I'd brought, creating an aureole around her hair, shining through the white shirt she wore as a smock to reveal (I was able to note in a sequence of stolen glances) the faint shadow of her breast beneath the light fabric as she leaned over to reorganize her implements, to select another pen, to pick up a piece of charcoal or graphite, continuing the studies in another medium, trying different effects to translate later into paint, asking me now and again to change the direction of my gaze, the two of us chatting easily, casually, me sipping wine with my eyes cast in the latest requested direction, sharing laughter with her at this or that joke made by one or the other of us, the sun hastening too swiftly on its afternoon course, creating in the wine roseate subtleties that are gone before they can fully be savoured, and sparkling briefly on the glass whose stem she curls her fingers delicately round, lifting it to her lips, sunlight thinning soon to dim hues of late afternoon, barely time to note the faint shadow of her breast beneath the light fabric of the shirt she wears for a smock, through which light glances, sun sinking fast after touching briefly upon her hair, creating a momentary halo, shadows entering the room, into which cooking odours have found their way, blending with the pungent smells of paint and turpentine, amid which, for the last fifteen minutes or so of natural light, she had had me relax and look wherever I wanted (mostly away from her, but much at her) while she flash-sketched and we exchanged inconsequential remarks about trivial matters...so pleasant a time, so trying an ordeal, so casual her manner, so strained my nerves, so sweet her demeanour, so painful the thought of her, so delightful her smile, so crucial to get out of there, so tempting her appearance, so essential to restrain myself, so promising her smiles, so foolish to succumb to them, so lingering her looks, so weak my resistance, so strong my desire, so short the afternoon, so long the time it seemed she took to shower and change while I smoked and lolled in the living room, listening to music on record or radio, until she returned and slipped down beside me on the couch in a sheath dress whose indigo colour set off the bright red of the small carnation pinned just at her cleavage, which flower she invited me to smell as she slid down beside my chair, holding a long-stemmed rose up to my face, saying, "Sniff," the platinum sleeve of her silk lounge suit sliding down her arm and the gentle aroma of perfume at her wrist mingling with the odour of the proffered blossom, the room awash in odours, the music soothing, her other hand resting lightly on my knee, lingering there briefly as she passes by me on her way round the counter at which I sit on a stool, sipping the scotch she poured and handed to me before putting on an apron to protect her bulky wool sweater from spatters or spills while she stirred this and ladled that and bent over to lift something out of the oven, causing her sweater, which hung almost to mid-thigh, to ride up at the back a little on her black leotards, revealing a hint of buttock from which I averted my eyes, because we were simply two people who had had an affair and would now have a dinner and would leave it at that, in spite of the hard-on I felt begin as she entered the shower, a clear glass stall to the left of the stage, inside which she stood in a white cotton dress with a full skirt, belted at the waist, just the trace of a smile on her lips as she executes a little spin to lift her skirt some and show a bit more leg, viewing through the glass the effect on her audience, her head tilted to her raised right shoulder as she runs her hands down her dress, pressing it close to emphasize the contours of her figure and imply a hint of autoeroticism, then reaches out to turn on the water that descends in a stream, under which she luxuriates, rolling her head back as the water soaks her white dress, making it transparent where it clings to her breasts and buttocks and thighs and back, and she pulls it tight at her crotch to reveal the dark triangle there, and moves without regard to the rhythms of the music that plays—irrelevantly, incongruously—peeling off her dress with tantalizing delays, at last to stand revealed in wet and naked glory, motionless, inviting, then slowly raises her arm to lift the showerhead out of its bracket and spray the glass to clear the obscuring mist and drops of water that have gathered on it, after which she turns and lavishes upon me a full and extended view of her buttocks, with much rolling and bending and pushing out to render visible the orifices harboured there, pressing herself against the glass, aiming the spray into her crotch, turning around and adjusting the nozzle until it emits a single, pulsing, concentrated jet that she directs towards the nipple of her left breast, cupped and kneaded with languorous sensuality, her nipple stiffening with the sustained stimulation, her smile broadening with the increased gratification, the procedure repeated on the other breast, the nozzle readjusted to a gentler flow that she plays over her vulva, pulling the lips apart to let the water stimulate her clitoris, her head thrown back now, her smile replaced by an urgent expression of frowning intensity, mouth an *o* of straining desire, body taut between the constrictive walls of the shower stall, head pressed to one panel, knees to another, fingers delving, water coursing, legs trembling, self convulsed in a rippling surrender to orgasmic reflex, as I hear the taps turned off upstairs and then the sounds of her walking around some, silence, footsteps, silence again (longer this time), footsteps again, silence and footsteps alternating for various durations, until I hear her descending the stairs and she enters, fresh and perfumed, in loose gray slacks and burgundy blouse, smiling and asking, "Hungry?"

I blame the candles (so long since I'd had a candlelit meal); I blame the meal (thick cream soup, a subtly spiced casserole, a bottle of wine); I blame the wine (a vintage Burgundy, the last of which we sipped on the living-room couch); I blame the couch (plush and comfortable, inducing a lassitude augmented by the classical guitar music playing on the stereo); I blame the stereo (at the end of the record the room filled with silence); I blame the silence (breathing a faint sigh, she leaned her head on the back of the couch, where I'd stretched out my arm); I blame my arm (lifting it a little as a prelude to removing it, I caused her head to roll slightly towards me and saw her smile); I blame her smile (it increased the flutter in my stomach, the trembling in my hands, the shortness of my breath, the dryness of my mouth, the pounding of my heart); I blame my heart.

Just a sort of farewell frolic (I told myself, as I left her house the next morning)—the kind of thing that often happens between former lovers when a relationship has effectually ended, a kind of tapering-off effect, nothing really...or not much: just a little spurt, a grappling, a grasping, a brief reprise of a show-stopping tune, a little nostalgic indulgence, a glance towards the past, a minor variation on a major theme, an ephemeral response to an animal impulse, an epilogue, a coda, a friendly fuck, a goodbye. Goodbye, Blackie. Goodbye.

15

She called a week later. The sitting was great. The studies were perfect—as far as they went. But she felt that she needed me just once more, for a *je ne sais quoi* that she wanted to capture, working directly to canvas this time. And she knew I was curious: no need to worry, she'd show me the painting. But when she was ready. Or rather, she meant, when the painting was ready. And really it would be, very soon now, it was coming along fantastically. Could I come next week? Pick my day. Thursday? Around nine p.m.? Fine. And I went, with a bottle of cognac in hand, and some flowers I'd picked up from a street vendor parked behind a little stand ranked with assorted bunches—roses, chrysanthemums, marigolds—throwing down a couple of dollars and grabbing the cellophane-wrapped bouquet, then dashing over to her place, ignoring the importunate whores outside the Barbados—sad, unbecoming women, caked with makeup, decked out in cheap, tight-fitting dresses that were supposed to fire off, in the hungry male mind, fantasies of wanton lust, forbidden pleasure amid silken opulence, easy virtue surrendered willingly in a mist of soft fabric and softer flesh: pitiful girls, of no real sexuality, asking incongruously, "Want a date, mister?" as though they'd never had a date in their lives and the surreptitious fuck in some seedy walk-up crib, or the quick blow job in a car down a dark lane, would make up for that, and the few bucks they earned would compensate them for the beatings they endured from dissatisfied pimps who thought they should have made more: "Fuckin' bitch! Y're holdin' back on me, ain'tcha? Ain'tcha?!" and back on the street with more bruises, now even less appealing and still less capable of making the expected amount, and on and on until they wind up god knows where, scrounging in some slum or wandering the streets with all their earthly possessions in shopping bags...past that and past the tinselly, raucous, good-timing, colour-lit atmosphere of the Barbados, where a guy leaned over to me at my table to ask, "Want a woman?" and I said, "No," thinking to myself, No, thinking, I don't want "a" woman, I want "the" woman, I want *her*, I want Black Satin, whatever her real name is, I want her: I want the elegant, intelligent, witty, warm, beautiful, sensitive, giving human being I imagine and believe her to be, opening her door and beaming with pleasure at the bottle and the flowers and ushering me in and looking more closely at the bottle and frowning, saying, "V.S.? Not V.S.O.P.? *V.S.!* You fucking cheapskate! And these chintzy little mums are bruised! What'd you pay for them—a buck? You couldn't go to a flower shop for cut mums? Jee-zus! Holy Christ, I get the real fuckin' pips, don't I? Absolutely fucking choice, you are. V.S...." while I stand there with a hangdog expression and cringe when she slaps the flowers across my chest, flinch when she smashes the bottle on the front walk, hasten to get the vacuum cleaner for the petals on the carpet and a broom and dustpan for the glass on the walk when she hollers, "Are you just going to stand there in your mess or clean it up, for chrissake? Am I supposed to live in a pigsty because of you?...Oh god!...Hose down the walk before you're finished, will you? I can't stand the smell of cheap brandy...If you ever get finished, you'll find me having an Armagnac in the studio—where you're *not* welcome, but where I want you to call out to me to let me know you're leaving."

She called a week later. The sitting was great. The studies were perfect—as far as they went. But she felt that she needed me just once more, for a *je ne sais quoi* that she wanted to capture, working directly to canvas this time. And she knew I was curious: no need to worry, she'd show me the painting. But when she was ready. Or rather, she meant, when the painting was ready. And really it would be, very soon now, it was coming along fantastically. Could I come next week? Pick my day. Thursday? Around nine p.m.? Fine. And I went, with a bottle of Armagnac in hand and an orchid, to which gifts she responded with a dubious look and a hesitant "Ohhh...," setting them on the coffee table and saying, "Look, maybe we should have a little talk, first. Uhmm, about last week...uh...I think you may have taken it a little more seriously than you should have. I mean these gifts are lovely, but really, don't you think it would be better if we just stayed friends? You're very sweet and I do appreciate this, but—well, I didn't mean to lead you on and if I did, then I don't want to lead you on any more and I think it would put things on a false footing if I were to accept these, so...No, please, don't insist. You take them when you go. We'll just do the sitting—I only need one more—and I'll show you the painting and...we'll keep in touch, okay?"

She called a week later. The sitting was great. The studies were perfect—as far as they went. But she felt that she needed me just once more, for a *je ne sais quoi* that she wanted to capture, working directly to canvas this time. And she knew I was curious: no need to worry, she'd show me the painting. But when she was ready. Or rather, she meant, when the painting was ready. And really it would be, very soon now, it was coming along fantastically. Could I come next week? Pick my day. Thursday? Around nine p.m.? Fine. And I went, with a bottle of fairly decent Chablis and a little nosegay of pansies and marigolds, which she accepted with a delighted smile, saying, "For me?" and I told her no, for the mailman, and she giggled and gave me a kiss and a hug, put the wine in the fridge to cool, set the blossoms in a flower dish on the kitchen table, and led the way to her studio, saying she didn't know if she was shy or superstitious, but she didn't want to show the painting to anyone until it was finished, did I mind? And of course I didn't: whatever she wanted; it was her painting and I was just an insignificant model; and she giggled and gave me a kiss, saying, "You're significant," and my heart melted. She worked for three hours without a break, having me relax my pose occasionally and at one point sending me to the kitchen for the wine, which was about the only time she spoke, holding a silence that I honoured, as she painted and paused and referred to sketches, working her palette awhile, approaching me closely and peering from different angles, painting some more, pausing, painting, and finally putting her brush down with a sigh, saying, "It's late. I'm tired. You've got work tomorrow. I

thought I'd be finished, but I'm not. Shit." My assurance that
I didn't mind a further sitting failed to lift her deflated mood,
for which she apologized, saying she always got this way when
her work didn't go as well as she'd like, then cleaning her
brushes, sitting with me in the living room while she finished
her glass of wine, trying to be sociable, thanking me for all my
time and my patience, unsure of when we could arrange the
next sitting because she had two weeks of road dates and then
a pile of work in the clubs around town, she really needed the
money right now, and maybe we could squeeze some time in
during her in-town dates, managing a smile as she kissed me
good-night at the door, from which kiss I broke, saying, "I
don't feel well." "Huh?" she responded, frowning slightly in
puzzled concern. "Yeah," I continued, "I don't know if it was
maybe something I ate earlier, but I don't feel very good, I
don't think I'm gonna be able to go to work tomorrow."
"Ohhh," she said, solicitously, "you want something to settle
your stomach, or—" "No," I replied, "it feels like it'll probably
go away on its own, although it is the kind of thing that I've
heard can be cured by a good night's sleep followed by expo-
sure to oil-paint fumes" (she looked perplexed) "so maybe if I
could come back tomorrow to sit for you, since I won't be in
the office..." The penny finally dropped and she laughed, her
face lighting up, and "Oh! *Would* you? Oh, if you could that'd
be so great. Really, I'm sure I could finish it tomorrow and
then I could go on the road feeling so much better. Oh, you're
such a darling! Are you sure you won't get into trouble at the
office?...No?...Positive?...Okay! Oh, listen—we could get a
nice early start if...if you stayed...?" leaning into my arms and
walking me back to the living room to pick up our wine-

glasses and to the kitchen to pick up the Chablis and up the stairs to her bedroom, where she lit the two small candles she always had burning whenever she made love, saying, "Makes it nicer, doesn't it? More romantic...sexxxier," drawing out that sibilance in the middle of the word "sexier," welcoming me into her arms, wriggling down with her head between my legs and arranging herself with my head between hers, everything rearranged again later, when we were both ready, her with her legs lifted and bent at the knees, in a kind of fetal position that allowed me to enter her, soon after which she splayed her legs, grasping her feet with her hands and rocking back and forth, moaning and panting and whispering words of endearment, both of us clutching at each other, our eyes fixed wide and eager, no image of my mother springing involuntarily to mind as we strain in our moaning, heaving, gasping, grunting con-junction—two human beings, slippery with sweat and blood and amniotic fluid, that is, I mean, vaginal juices and seminal fluid, crying out in pain, or rather, surprise, pulling me from her, although of course, no, guiding me into her...oh, nothing like my mother either physically or temperamentally...in no way reminding me of my mother, who would never cry out, "Fuck me! Fuck me! Oh Jesus, yes, fuck me! Oh God, you fuck so good! Oh, fuck me, *fuck me*, FUUUUUUUUUUU-UUCK!" that not being her mode of expression, though it certainly was Blackie's, which was one of the things my moth-er wouldn't have liked about her, aside from the fact that I was falling in love with her—I mean with Blackie, not my moth-er. I wasn't falling in love with my mother, although I did love her. I was falling in love with Blackie and my mother would-n't have liked that. She never did like it whenever I fell in love with anyone, not that I ever did really, however much I might have thought so, not that I'd let her know whenever I did think so, not that I could stop her from knowing, not that I could stop myself from falling in love with Blackie, not that I was falling in love with Blackie, I'd just gone to bed with her after that one sitting, that's all, a single little incident, a bit of backsliding, perfectly understandable, perfectly natural, not to be given a second thought: she'd done her sketches that Sunday, and when the painting was finished she'd give me a call to come have a look at it and I would compliment her on it and toast her with the Chardonnay I'd brought and she would thank me for the sitting and tell me she was planning to hang the painting in the group exhibit she had coming up, the opening of which I would attend, sipping wine and making conversation with the people I knew there, congratulating her and hugging her warmly, giving a little kiss goodbye before leaving, walking off into the night, feeling glad that the show was a success, knowing I'd see her now and again, keep up the friendship, follow her successes, gradually lose track of her, remember her fondly from time to time, miss her a little perhaps, forget her.

I called a week later. How had the sitting been? Fine, she said. Just great, in fact. The studies were perfect. She'd been after a kind of a *je ne sais quoi* that she'd managed to capture and transfer to canvas. She'd thought for a while that she might have to ask me to do a second sitting, but no, it had all worked out fine. The painting was finished, had come along fantastically. Well, could I see it? What?...Oh...Yeah...Sure. But she was going out of town for a couple of weeks to do road dates and had a heavy schedule in clubs around town after that, so we might have trouble setting up a time. Well, I could be flexible, when was she back? In a couple of weeks, like she said. Well, but, two exactly, or three, or what? Why did I always have to be so precise? she wanted to know. She was out on the road for a while. What was the big deal? Did I own her? Well, no...I didn't own her...and I didn't want to own her...I just wanted to see the painting, for chrissake. I was interested in her work and I'd done my bit to help out on the thing and I just wanted to see how it turned out. Yeah, well, okay, she was really kind of busy with getting ready for the road dates and everything, so maybe she could just get on with that and when she got back she'd give me a call or something, okay? Well, yeah, sure, but...listen, I was just calling up out of interest, I didn't mean to get her back up, I hadn't intended anything to get testy over—Just what did I mean saying she was testy? Aw, look, c'mon...I just was interested and wanted to see the painting. If she was coming up to her period or something and was irritable—Period!? Coming up to her period?! What the hell was I driving at with that sexist bullshit? Well, no...it wasn't "sexist bullshit," I was just trying to be understanding...Yeah, well, if I wanted to be understanding maybe I could understand that she had a lot on her plate right now and had a road trip to contend with, like immediately, so she would really like to get on with that and maybe she could just call me when things settled down, okay? Well, sure...okay...hope the road trip's not too bad...Yeah. Thanks. See ya. Click. Bye.

◆　◆　◆

"Hi! How ya doin'?"

"Oh, hi, Blackie. Fine. How're you?"

"Great—I finished the painting! It looks fabulous! Wanna see it?"

"Well, yeah, sure, of course! When can I come over?"

"Right now. You free?"

"I wasn't, but I am now. See you in a few minutes."

"Great! Hurry! Oh, I'm so excited!"

◆　◆　◆

A kaleidoscope of eyes, executed in various styles, viewed from numerous angles: eyes singly and in pairs; eyes with only lids and lashes; eyes within the space from brow to mid-cheek, as though the horizontal black band of anonymity, sometimes applied by wary publishers of cheap scandal sheets to subjects photographed in some scurrilous activity, were reversed to reveal only that portion of the person initially obliterated; eyes angry and eyes sad; eyes pensive, seductive, squinting, sparkling, bespectacled, goggled, staring, droopy-lidded; an eye under surgery—lids tied back, scalpel incising; eyes with their musculature exposed, eyes behind veils, eyes lowered, eyes raised, eyes of every hue and age, male eyes, female eyes, evil eyes, my eyes in the centre of the painting, in great glopping mounds of oils, raised thereby in relief, the rest of the canvas done in even, level application...my eyes, imbued with a quality of aching intensity, somehow ambiguous, vulnerable yet guarded, as though on the verge of great anger or great sadness, eyes I'd never have known as mine were it not for their having a fuller facial setting than any other pair of eyes in the

painting: my brow and hairline, my protuberant ears, my upper
cheeks, my nose with the tiny scar on its bridge, my eyes not
as I knew them, not fired with confidence and purpose, not
twinkling with humour, not charged with sexual desire, but
quizzical, yearning, dubious, worried almost...eyes I would
never claim as mine, eyes that couldn't be mine: she had
worked from fancy and fabrication, had used the sketches only
for details of facial structure, had not painted my eyes, had
made a fiction, had "...managed to capture some of your
intensity, don't you think? God, you have intense eyes...kinda
sexy actually. I think I got that—and the depth. Well...say
something. C'mon." "It's beautiful, Blackie...spectacular,"
which it was—in concept, composition, and execution—as
good as any and better than most in the local galleries, which
I told her, toasting her, assuring her that yes, I really believed
that; no, I wasn't just saying it to get her to go to bed with me;
yes, of course, I always wanted to go to bed with her—but I
wasn't praising her painting as a means of doing so; no, I did-
n't know that the creative and the sexual drives were apparently so closely linked as to be almost the same thing, but it
made sense when you thought about it, and yes, I'd say she
certainly was in a highly creative phase, so yes, I could understand that she—

When we arose from her studio couch, an old relic sal-
vaged from some outdoors location, with cushions that had
responded to the demands we placed upon them by issuing
little puffs of dust from the depths of their soiled stuffings,
Blackie insisted, for the sake of her sheets, that we take show-
ers before retiring, preferring me to go first while she tidied
up some in the kitchen, so I ascended to the bathroom,

removed my dishevelled clothes, and, upon turning to hang them on a hook on the back of the door, found myself facing a full-length mirror, looking straight into my eyes imbued with a quality of aching intensity, somehow ambiguous, vulnerable yet guarded, as though on the verge of great anger or great sadness, eyes I'd never have known as mine were it not for my brow and hairline, my protuberant ears, my upper cheeks, my nose with the tiny scar on its bridge, my eyes not as I knew them, not fired with confidence and purpose, not twinkling with humour, not charged with sexual desire, but quizzical, yearning, dubious, worried almost...eyes I would never claim as mine, eyes worked from fancy and fabrication, eyes I could not see as sexy, whose depth eluded me, eyes pensive, eyes staring, eyes reversed to reveal only that portion of the person initially obliterated, eyes behind a veil, evil eyes, my eyes, red-rimmed and stinging, revealing the person, yearning and quizzical, dubious, worried, turning from the mirror, from my eyes bared, soul seers seeing me in mirror turning, on the verge of great anger or great sadness, water streaming down my face beneath the shower tap turned on to wash burning eyes squeezed tight against the hot stream causing my shoulders to shake, a hand against the tiled wall, head bent forward, mouth convulsed in silent sobs, other hand at brow, eyes shut against their image persisting behind them, pained eyes, other eyes, her eyes, any eyes but my eyes I couldn't deny, the ache in them in me, a sadness and anger unravelling from cabled muscles shaking soft in body wet and sinking under shower stream to sag on tile floor and slowly rise with hand to soap rack reaching, dropping slack again and shoulders shaking, listless head on chest, and flood abating, slowly start to soap myself, and hear her enter the bathroom, saying, "Just coming to make sure you wash behind your ears," and opening the shower door, smiling and asking, "Room for one more?"

As we dried each other after our shower, standing in clouds of diminishing steam, she turned me around to towel my back, facing me towards the sink, and I saw, through the moisture condensed on the mirror above it, the vague outlines of our shapes towards which her hand reached to wipe away the film at eye level, her voice at my ear whispering, "Look at those eyes!...Oh-h-h-h-h-h!...So intense!...Sex-yyy..." and I looked intensely, trying to see what she saw, seeing only pathetic little puppy-dog eyes with a doleful please-don't-hit-me expression, wary eyes, worried eyes, eyes looking to please, eyes wanting something, eyes filled with bemusement, with, perhaps, a kind of concern, as though not really sure what it is that's required of them but eager to do whatever it is, eyes with small pools gathering at the lower lids, eyes that close when I feel her mouth on my neck, moving across my cheek, up to my eyes, and I turn to hold her, feeling a drop of the stomach, as though her presence before me creates an absence within me, to which I surrender and feel myself fill with fear and a surge of emotion I try to give voice to, trying to speak, saying, "I—" and choking, trying again, saying, "I-I..." over breaking breath, stammering, "I-I-I...l-luh-..." breath gone and gasping in more to push out "l-l-l-love..." then a trembling intake and choking with sobs on the "y-y-y-ou-ouu-ouuuu!" collapsing against her, clutching her, weeping, her hands holding my head and caressing it, lips kissing my eyes, voice breathing, "It's all right...It's all right..."

16

She was just as I wanted her, always wanted her wildcat blonde
hair hanging just past her left shoulder, towards which her
head was tilted, almost horizontal, her gaze lascivious, her pose
provocative, right leg lifted with heel on couch, weight supported by left hand and left buttock, left leg outstretched,
crotch displayed, sheer blue blouse open and hanging to either
side of her torso, which is twisted slightly as she peers back
over her right shoulder to view the effect that her raised posterior has on me, her weight supported by her hands on the
bed, her body bent at the waist, her feet on the floor in spiked
high-heeled slippers, great breasts pendulous, nipples erect,
cunt moist between lifted legs held up from the poolside tiles,
black hair sprayed out across the ceramic surface, eyes closed
in rapture, hands cupping the tiny breasts whose jutting nipples I will lower my mouth to where she pulls at the stiff dark
flesh whose folds she will spread with fingers reaching back to
open the warm cavity from which will seep moisture damp-
ening the red hairs curling round my lips sucking at the pink

puckers with darkened pigment she lifted from the sand of the beach she'd squatted on, pulling the crotch of her white bathing suit aside and hugging her knees in a kind of fetal position, her blue-gray eyes holding a dare or challenge, her sandy hair gathered from the neck and piled atop her head tilted inquisitively to one side of her left buttock pulled up by her left hand reaching to scratch her nose, a pert little protuberance with a sprinkle of freckles across it, reddish-brown splotches of spreading liver spots on the back of a wrinkled hand she wipes across sagging lids over brown eyes red-rimmed above bulging pouches beside the hook of her nose, from the apertures of which protrude tiny curling hairs, white commas and quotation marks that punctuate the syntax of time she proclaims in the stretched flesh of her bunioned feet she shifts on the rung of the stool that supports her weight at the bar, beer in hand, bare lower back beneath midriff halter top and hip-high skirt, pale band of flesh between, torso twisted, bent to the right, intent on friend's talk, bent intent right to pale band of friend's talk, bare bar of flesh between halter and skirt top, hip-swell, standing in mid-thigh spandex shorts, T-shirt to mid-bum, sandy hair mid-back, thigh-high skirt, brown hair ponytailed just beneath shoulder lowered to let drop strap of blood-red bra her breasts spill out of, hazel eyes sparking a challenge, streaked hair curled, straight line of long nose nearly touching top of full lip lifted in laughter, eyebrows arched over bedroom-eyes blue, blonde hair braided to one side falling over small breasts strawberry-tipped, peach-fuzz hair I lip, bruised blue love bite, stretching to tilt her head to shrugged shoulder hair descends to, straight leg in sheer white stocking hooked by garter strap strung from frilled belt around waist creased with stretch marks, straight black hair lowered to strawberry-tipped peach fuzz on her right leg lifted with her feet on eyebrows arched over sheer white stockings hooked by tiny curling hairs standing in red-rimmed spandex shorts I will lower my mouth to stretch marks straight from the apertures at mid-thigh that her shrugged shoulder descends to slender foot in a kind of fetal position at the bar the burnished black of her thigh with a sprinkle of freckles across the ceramic surface of her crotch displayed with moisture that will dampen the folds of her white bathing suit twisted to mid-bum above the cream-coffee flesh of her eyes closed to knees tilted inquisitively atop nipples sucking at pink hair curled to either side of the beach between left hand and left buttock on the rung of the stool sucking at the pert little protuberance that will seep to the right of her blue-gray eyes intent on talk of dope she wants to score, gray hair straggling from the edges of her woolen toque worn through the summer, begging coins for booze, reaching a slender hand for a cigarette, silver bracelet clinking on marble bar, asking how much the cocaine will cost, the zipper of her spangled dress undone, mischievous smile as she removes her bra to reveal her breasts that will bounce and wrinkle and sag and finding a vein to insert the needle in just one more bottle of whisky passed out on the lawn in front of some halfway house that won't accept her flesh pierced by a piece of metal left there by the cabby who she has no money for just a toke through bruised lips someone hit what's left is not right how I wanted her just as I wanted her to leer as she lifted her breasts with her right forearm pierced by a tiny piece of metal where she would smile at some bon mot the bartender makes in spandex shorts hugging her knees as she sits on the grass she can't afford but wants just one more joint to get there to the only thing she ever wanted was a way out of the mess she found herself in nothing but a flimsy negligee before an appreciative audience her sloe face will rise above the eyes fixed on the body flung against the ropes strung around the stage the owner pounds on when the two of them are closer than the law allows their genitals to be private property on public view the one has of the other pinned on the mat the referee pounds on once and twice when suddenly the one that's under stops the simulated cunnilingus everyone's intent upon the body slam from mid-ring back to the rope her body leans against while anxious owner pounds the stage when lips approach her nipple closer than the hand that grabs the hair and whacks at eyes of outraged manager across the ring of flesh on bum that's bruise or birthmark referee's oblivious to spandex-covered knee in eye they break the hold they had and pull the G-string off the colours of their cunts are the syntax of time that's lost in the joint bent nearly double standards applying ointment to the injured muscle hit by the needle that missed the vein of humour in some point of honour lost in silver threads among the gold band circling her ankle thick and foot flat in sensible shoe her arch is fallen back on a proscenium she lifts her bum from showing pimple on perineum my tongue will lick the white hair round the wrinkled flesh her eyelids are lowered in provocative pose she assumes I love her and I do.

17

Shortly after I said I wanted to move in with her she said she
wanted to move in with me or shortly after she said she wanted to move in with me I said I wanted to move in with her or
anyway we said we wanted to move in together, and she
moved in with me or I moved in with her or we moved
together somewhere I remember moving in a closet of her
clothes. She moved in with me or I moved in with her or we
moved in with each other in each other's places, since she
owned hers and I rented mine at a price so cheap we didn't
want to give it up, a place where I could go when I wanted to
be alone or when she wanted to be alone, so she moved partly in with me, or I moved partly in with her, moving in some
clothes, I seem to remember, her clothes and mine in a closet
at my place or hers, where I'd moved in a few things at her
suggestion after, I think, the day I had to go into the office
from her place wearing a suit that had got something spilled
on it and I'd overslept and had no time to get to my place, dash
in, change, skip breakfast, return for my briefcase, return again

to get the papers that I suddenly remembered were on my desk, buck traffic all the way to the office, and barely arrive on time for my meeting, planning on the way there my excuses for being late to meet my boss's glare for arriving on time in a soiled suit or for arriving late in a fresh one, which Blackie'd taken from my closet, saying, "This'll knock 'em out! Wear this! C'mon, I'll help you put it on...First the right leg: there's the boy...and now the left: that's it! Now here: we'll do the button up and zip the fly and pull the belt tight and buckle it. Okay, stand up and we'll put on our jacket. That's the way: left arm first and now the right. Oh! Handsome!...And a hanky in the breast pocket," which I pull out during the meeting, at which coffee's been served, to wipe some drops from my moustache, and find the smell of her juices on the underpants she's tucked in there and quickly shove them into my inside jacket pocket, as my boss lowers her eyelids briefly and then glances up and to the side, lips pursed, glaring at me through-out the meeting, the visiting executives either not noticing or pretending not to notice that the pair of Blackie's panties that I carry in my inside jacket pocket as a kind of charm or memento have just fallen into my lap in the course of my extracting from my inside pocket the notepad I usually carry in my side pocket but that I had, in my hurry that morning, shoved into the pocket where I always keep, for the purpose of conjuring her presence by fondling and sniffing them, a pair of her panties, which I now surreptitiously slip into my side pants pocket, not daring to glance to my right, where my boss sits, briefly closing her eyes in exasperation, rolling them ceil-ingwards, pulling her mouth down at the side and breathing a slow, barely perceptible sigh, the whole episode resulting in an

unaccustomed lack of concentration on my part, so that I
missed some numbers I should have written down and twice
asked about matters that had already been thoroughly covered,
the second time in the high-class restaurant we'd gone to for
lunch, where I reached into my pants pocket for my lighter
and noticed one of the visiting executives making a little
"tsch" sound and shaking his head slightly, which I thought
nothing of until a few minutes later, when a waiter stopped
beside me and leaned over to whisper discreetly, "Excuse me,
sir, but I think you dropped something," pointing to the carpeted floor beside me, where I looked to find Blackie's red silk
panties lying beside my chair and leant down as nonchalantly
as possible to snatch them up and shove them into my hip
pocket, from which they slid out a few days later, to lie on the
clothes-closet floor at my place or Blackie's, where she found
them and picked them up, saying, "Here they are! I've been
looking for these. How'd they get here?" which I could have
told her but decided not to, wondering if she'd peel off her
evening gown during her act some night and find one of my
socks lying on the stage, which never did happen, I think,
though I believe she did once mention something to me
about being more careful where my ties wound up, beyond
which there was never any confusion with each other's
clothes, except for the time that I realized, just before the
hoots of derision would have arisen in the dressing room, that
I was about to don one of her black lace garter belts to hold
up my hockey socks.

Not that we ever dressed up in each other's clothes. She
would not, for instance, don a three-piece suit and, with me
decked out in a sheath dress and scanty underthings, do a mash

job on me, pinch my ass while I made dinner, stand behind me later at the sink and nuzzle my neck while I sighed and said, "Oh, you...Not just yet...Let me finish the dishes..." which of course she wouldn't, being so male and domineering, sliding her hands over my thighs and lifting my skirt, which I would push back down to a modest level, trying to fend her off without crushing her fragile male ego, not wanting to be so adamant that she wouldn't try again nor so compliant that she'd think me easy and lose respect for me, feeling myself getting all moist and mushy as I caught a whiff of her cologne, hoping she was getting aroused by my perfume, worried that I'd either applied so little that it was imperceptible or so much that it was overwhelming, making me seem a cheap little tart, too eager for that swelling roll of salami I could feel straining between my buttocks and against which I rubbed my ass up and down, finally abandoning the dishes to turn around and sink to my knees, unbuckling the belt, unzipping the fly, tugging my bodice down to let my tits pop out so I could squeeze that big hard cock between them until the come squirted out on my chin and I lowered my mouth to lick and suck the already subsiding rod, hoping to keep it stiff, panting and whimpering as it was pulled out of my mouth and I could feel myself lifted, eyes closed, onto the kitchen counter, my sheath dress hiked up so it was just a roll of fabric around my waist, my flimsy little soaked panties ripped off and flung to the floor, my legs lifted up and pushed apart so my cunt was open and vulnerable to the delicious probings of an expert tongue that periodically darted down to flick briefly at my asshole, sending lingering thrills through my whole nervous system, the tongue redoubling its efforts at my cunt, until I threw my head back and screamed and shook in rippling orgasm, hardly completed before I found myself thrust forward over the kitchen table with the thick plunging shaft of a hot wet cock pumping furiously inside my dripping hole.

Nor would she occasionally dress up in my hockey equipment—except for the skates—and stride into the bedroom, where I lounged in negligee, bra, and panties, reading a home-design magazine that she flicked out of my hands with the hockey stick she then flung aside, striking a commanding pose, hands on hips, before provocatively peeling off the gear: sweater, elbow pads, shoulder pads, pants, and jock, wearing no long johns or undershirt, just the socks with the shin guards tucked in them and, in place of the sturdy hockey garter belt, a frilly black one from her own wardrobe, which would have accounted for the item that wound up in my equipment that day at the rink—and which the guys never did let me live down, riding me about it almost every week thereafter—except that she never did do anything like that, with or without her own garter belt, marching into the bedroom wearing work clothes and steel-capped boots, looking mean and single-purposed, throwing a scare into me by wordlessly ripping off my negligee and tearing it into strips while I cowered on the bed, meekly protesting as she used the shreds of the garment to gag and tie me, spread-eagled on the bed, taking me roughly and perfunctorily, grunting once when she was through, doing up her pants and departing for some lowlife pub to swill beer with her cronies, leaving me bound to the bed, weeping quietly and desperately, my mouth chafed by the gag, praying that when she came home drunk she wouldn't be in too vindictive a mood and would, just maybe, untie me before slipping into the snoring coma with which she always concluded such nights, nights that left me physically and emotionally drained, so that the next day at the office was torture to get through, made worse by the curious glances my co-workers cast at my fresh bruises, and worse still by the occasional remark made about the bruises, which remarks I would brush off with some trumped-up story about a domestic accident or a bit of rough-and-tumble at hockey, which games Blackie liked to attend when her schedule permitted, asking me not to shower after because, funny as it seemed, and not that it would work on a regular basis, but sometimes, after watching me play, the pungent odour of male animal (as she called it) was a special kind of turn-on for her in bed, at which times—and only at which times—she would ask me to be a little rough with her, roughness something that neither of us were prone to, other than the occasional destruction of a piece of clothing when one or the other of us lost patience with buttons or clasps.

It was as much my going out drinking with the guys after hockey as her attending spontaneous parties after working in the clubs that created friction between us, although, as I was at pains to point out, there was less chance of me winding up in bed with one of the guys from hockey than there was of her winding up in bed with someone from one of her after-work parties, which I argued about with her over and over in my mind, never voicing it aloud because I knew there was nothing to be gained by that, nothing but further friction between us about her in the embrace of some muscular left-winger I imagined with his arm around me over a beer in the pub, leading to another beer in the pub, and then another, and then what the hell, why not another back at his place with the rest of the gang that dwindled away till there was just the two of us, our intimate conversation soon leading to physical intimacy, innocent enough at first, his hand briefly on my thigh, which she takes no notice of at first, so intent on the topic of conversation, until he's gradually got it under her skirt and we're suddenly further along with things than she'd ever intended, her hormones reacting at a level she can't control, his hand touching me knowingly, tenderly, expertly, just back of my balls and forwards along, thrilling soft sensations the lengths of the nerves there, giving pleasure I hadn't thought I'd experience at the touch of a man she suddenly wants with an impulsive intensity that obliterates me from her mind whose only focus is the hand that now unbuckles the belt and undoes the jeans and reaches inside the underwear as his tongue slips between my teeth and flicks over her tongue responding feverishly to the heat of the moment in which everything's out of control except our mouth on that swelling purple helmet we want inside us so badly we'd do anything to have his finger pushing into the moist orifice his tongue probes so insistently, lifting up the fleshy hood to lick at the erect organ so eager for the encounter that causes so much fiction between us, finally arriving at a compromise by which I will drive directly from hockey to whatever club she's at, where she will have gone by taxi, and we'll ride home together, her complaining all the way about the locker-room stench that pervades my car because I didn't have enough time to shower after hockey, "So? I'll wait a little longer! Take a fucking shower! You reek!"

But painting the exterior of the house sky-blue with puffy white clouds would only get the neighbours up in arms, I insisted, not that such an argument held any more water for her than her argument—that it was her house and she could do what she wanted with it—held for me. I was practically living there...or, anyway, I was partially living there...anyhow, it didn't matter whether I was practically living there or partially living there, I said, I was there a lot and I cared about her and I didn't want to see her getting into an ugly situation with her neighbours just because she made a joke about painting her house in army-camouflage brown-and-olive and I said, "Why not sky blue with puffy clouds?" and she laughed and then thought a bit and said that actually sounded like a neat idea, and I laughed, thinking she was just joking, or she laughed, thinking I was just joking, or we both laughed until I said maybe it wasn't such a bad idea and she said it was a terrible idea or maybe she said it wasn't such a bad idea and I said it was a terrible idea and I got adamant about it or she did, or at least, that's how I remember it, however accurate my memory may be, which I hope is accurate enough, although accurate enough for what, I can't say, I don't know, though I hope I might sometime, which I suspect will be the longest time, which is how long the argument about the painting of her house went on between us, punctuated by complaints about dishes left dirty in the kitchen, laundry undone and overflowing the hamper, finances disorganized, hair unkempt, body unwashed, clothes in disarray, studies neglected, nails untrimmed, beard ungroomed, career abandoned, sexuality stunted, chances missed, opportunities unpursued, correspondence unanswered, intellect undisciplined, bills unpaid, words misspelled, grammar inaccurate, manners forgotten, milk spilt, bed wet, food dribbled, pants shit: I was a recalcitrant infant, child, son, person, being—beneath contempt and beyond hope. And she whose image arises continually before me is, of course, not my mother, oh, certainly not my mother, so unlike the fragile, thin-limbed, frail-built woman who bore me, bred me, succoured and seduced me—no, I mean *re*duced me, that is, I mean *in*duced me, I mean *excused* me for having insisted on a blue sky with puffy white clouds as the wallpaper design for the room she let me have in her house she wanted me out of for a few days while she collected herself, she said, feeling a need to reclaim her own space, which was why we'd decided I'd keep my apartment, wasn't it?

Which was, of course, why we'd decided I'd keep my apartment, where I went for a few days, as Blackie requested, feeling rejected at first, but gradually coming to terms with that, realizing that I needed to reclaim my own space too, enjoying it finally, dropping in on her a few days later and finding her looking at a home-design magazine with a feature on nurseries, from which she glanced up at me to say, "I'm pregnant."

18

Home in my easy chair, reading the paper, scotch on the rocks, and feet up at last, a violin solo by Bach playing low on the stereo, Blackie ensconced on the chesterfield opposite, nursing the baby, her head bent towards it, humming distractedly, immersed in the private universe of mother and child, beside which the news becomes so insignificant the paper slips onto my lap and, lifting my glass to sip, I gaze at the scene before me with a contented smile and a soft sigh, savouring the bouquet of household odours: the roast in the oven, the vegetables steaming, the warm, humid air of the living room (kept like that for the baby's sake). And the strength of my emotions causes my eyes to brim briefly with tears I press my lids against, raising my eyebrows to counter the squint before relaxing the muscles there, drifting into reverie, envisioning the nursery I'd spent months of spare time on, doing carpentry and lighting, panelling and painting, in constant consultation with Blackie to ensure that her wishes were met in every detail of the most important room in the house, a room furnished with cabinets for clothing and diapers, shelves for fluffy toy animals, a table for the bassinet, a crib with overhanging mobiles and fabric bangles on spring rods, the ceiling painted sky blue with little puffy clouds, one wall papered with a design of cuddly bear cubs and lambs and kittens and puppies, another panelled, the others painted pastel yellow, plush carpet on the floor, a rocking chair in the corner with a nursery lamp on the chifforobe beside it, a vaporizer set on the carpet, the room redolent of oils, lotions, powders, creams, and ointments, the odours of which seep into the other rooms, even, it seems, into the living room, where Blackie hums and nurses and I run over a mental inventory of precautionary devices I will be installing throughout the house—security gates, safety catches on cupboards in kitchen and bathroom, safety wall plugs, safety door locks—marvelling at how much pleasure I've derived from planning and working on every stage of things, finishing my drink and proceeding to the kitchen to get our dinner on the table, as Blackie ascends to the nursery with the baby, settling it for sleep while I mash potatoes and perfect the gravy, uncork the wine and arrange the table where she'd sat that day and made the announcement that left me momentarily speechless, until, whooping with delight, I threw my arms around her, lifted her laughing out of her chair, swung her round the room, set her back down, and stood there enjoying her glow, beaming back at her, enumerating the changes we'd make to welcome the child, pressing for details of the doctor's counsel, asking about my prenatal responsibilities, raising the prospect of home childbirth, envisioning a scene just such as this, with me putting dinner on the table as Blackie descends from the nursery and sits down, occupying the same chair as she had on the day that I heard her calm statement and felt the blood drain from my face and asked, in a croaking voice I barely recognized as mine, "Are you sure?"—at which she began to cry, saying through her tears, "Well, isn't that a wonderful response?" while I shifted from one foot to the other, biting my tongue to keep from asking what proof there was that the kid was mine, trying to quell my panic at the prospect of parenthood, every molecule screaming No! as I moved to placate her, which she would have none of, striking out at me as I went to put my arm around her, feeling abandoned, empty, helpless, overwhelmed by the choices on the menu of the high-class restaurant to which I'd taken her to celebrate, unable to decide between egg, veal, or lamb, hearing her chatter about the changes we'd have to make in our lives, the details of the doctor's counsel, her wish for a natural home childbirth with me in attendance, the head of the baby pushing through, the midwife issuing curt commands that I follow with confidence gained through reading and instruction during the prenatal period, the doctor's intense, efficient manner, the blood, the screams, the rare steak set before me as I inquire about whether there was any warning of dangers that could prevent the pregnancy coming to term, whereupon Blackie's face froze and, with eyes held on mine, she said, "You don't want this baby," which I assured her wasn't the case, I was delighted, really, I just wanted to know what dangers might be met, the better to avoid or offset them, and why was she making such a fuss, maybe it was she who didn't want the baby, in which case she should consider an abortion, at which she turned pale and, rising, announced that she was going to get a cab, from which I vainly tried to dissuade her, following her from the restaurant after throwing enough money on the table to appease the startled waiter, pleading with her all the way out the door of the restaurant and up to the cab that she silently entered and locked the door of, with me fumbling at the handle of the departing vehicle, forgetting the food untouched on the table, the roast I'd taken such care to prepare, the gravy done to perfection, the potatoes and vegetables turning cold as I wonder what's taking her so long in the nursery, why the baby is crying so, what she could be doing to it, poor defenseless little creature, utterly reliant on a woman filled with anger so palpable the kid would, if not bearing the brunt of it, surely sense its intensity, perhaps somehow believe itself to be the cause of it and, as a result, feel overwhelmed, empty, helpless, abandoned, a recalcitrant infant, child, person, being, with incalculable faults, inabilities, and failures in matters moral, social, physical, emotional, spiritual, and nutritional, of unfulfilled promise, unrealized talents, undisciplined intellect, hair unkempt, body unwashed, clothes in disarray, milk spilt, bed wet, food dribbled, pants shit—beneath contempt and beyond hope, always somehow managing, with instinct blind but unerring, to perpetrate just the enormity that would goad Blackie into a rage, get her to yank down the poor little kid's pants and pull it over her knee to slap its tiny bum red, so intent on her task that she doesn't even notice me enter the room until I've covered the distance from the door to her chair and grabbed her wrist to prevent the next blow from descending, confronting the mask of anger her face is set in, eyes burning at me as she twists and jerks her arm in an effort to get free of my grasp, determined to strike again, to overcome anything or anybody standing between her and her manifest intent, incredulous at my efforts to stop her, enraged by my suggestion that we not have the baby, screaming at me, "How could you? How could you? I hate you! I hate you!"—which I knew she didn't, really, it was just her frustration coming out, the kind of emotional instability women experience during pregnancy, with all kinds of irrational fears and radical mood swings: she just needed to let herself relax a bit and then we could simply discuss whether or not we really wanted to have the kid. It wasn't as though I was suggesting murder or anything: the embryo might already be incapable of actually being born, of even becoming a person—the thing was hardly more than a zygote, for god's sake. What was wrong with her? She was completely overreacting. I was behaving like she was a biology-class exhibit instead of a living person with a new life forming inside her. How could I be so inhuman? She must've been crazy to have ever loved me. What kind of monster was I? Which she knew I wasn't, of course—or, I should say, would've known even if I ever had suggested such a thing, not that I would've, not that I did, since I'm sure I wouldn't have, at least not explicitly; I mean, it might've crossed my mind, I might even have said something that might have seemed like that was what I was driving at, but I would never suggest any interference with what nature had set in motion, with what we had got going, growing there in the dark inside her where I'd helped put it, how (I mean at a cellular level, a chemical level) I don't know—or (perhaps more to the point) why or (even more, perhaps, to the point) when. Because we were apart for a while—I mean, we were living apart for a while...that is, we got together now and then and we, of course, made love because (of course) we hadn't broken up, we weren't really apart, we were only getting our separate spaces together and our separate spaces came together there in the dark in her from the dark in me and neither of us knew when or (I mean at a cellular level, a chemical level) how or (more, perhaps, to the point) why. And although we weren't really broken up, the pieces of us came together inside her there without our knowing it, to form, out of so many million possibilities, a fragile unit that slipped down the slender tube, stuck to the wall of the bulb lower down, and started growing.

Frankly, I'm still baffled by its doing so, by its forming at all in the first place, by one tiny sperm managing to make its way back in there through so many curves and crannies, with millions like it dying all around it and vast numbers of cilia waving the other way, to find that one-in-four-weeks egg at some point within less than twenty-four hours after the egg is ready and right there, to get to it just then, right near the top of that tube, in the exact place at the exact time, propelled by a sense of burning urgency on that one momentous evening, or afternoon, or whatever time of day it was that I abandoned some incidental, though not unimportant, undertaking and hastened to Blackie in response to, not a prurient whim, but a deep elemental call, an unconscious signal transmitted from somewhere within the depths of her on a frequency only I could receive, a signal that cut through the pervasive static characterizing my day-to-day existence, and drew that cell, with siren magnetism, to the dark fold where the egg nestled, to poke and prod until it got through the gelatinous outer layer and finally pierced the membrane of the egg and a few days later Blackie's breasts tingled and swelled and grew tender and her period didn't come as it usually did and she final-

ly went to her doctor and the test came back positive and we
would be parents and I was happy and proud and confused and
terrified and wanted it and didn't want it and don't, growing
there in the dark inside her, deepening the brown of her aure-
oles, creating blue and pink lines on her breasts, tiring her,
swelling her gums, pushing her guts all to hell and gone,
squashing them back and up and wrecking her digestion and
giving her heartburn and piles and constipation, none of
which she makes much of, taking it all in stride, including the
things (especially the things) that keep her from working: vas-
cular spiders, abdominal swelling, backache, leg cramps, lethar-
gy: the guys in the front row aren't too keen about all the
things their lust can lead to, liking their dancers lean and clean
and lively, barefoot and sterile on the runway...no varicose
veins, please, no swollen ankles, nothing that might bring to
mind things like contractions, episiotomies, blood, placentae,
babies. Sometimes I wonder why she does it, laying herself
open like that to titillate them, subjecting herself to their crit-
ical gaze and judgement, though if she didn't do it we'd probably never have met and we wouldn't be in this together,
which I wish we weren't, because I'm too young to be a
father, or too old, or too selfish, too stubborn, too vain, mean,
shallow, impudent, rude, materialistic, predatory, immoral,
undisciplined, prejudiced, impractical, deceitful, helpless, abandoned, overwhelmed, empty, ashamed of myself, of my swollen
extremities and morning sickness, my tender breasts, my errat-
ic moods, my bloated belly, my perpetual lust, my rapid weight
gain, my continual need to piss, my insomnia, tiredness, nose-
bleeds, itchiness, cravings, fear of ripping open when it wants
out, stopping painting to protect it from the fumes, special

exercises to make a flat stomach possible again when all this is over, stuffy nose, shortness of breath, worry about teratogens, proteinuria, gestational diabetes, placenta previa...and will I ever lie on my back again? How'd I get into this? Why'd the little fucker pick me? I'm just something to hold on to for what I can provide, a host to be leeched off, someone to "love," whatever that's supposed to mean: usually that the bastard lives off you somehow until you're no longer useful and you get left alone, helpless, empty, the thing torn out of you and everybody ooing and aahing for a few weeks or months and then forgetting about it, about you, about the whole enterprise, and I want it not to be and to be over with and never to end and to stop hurting, please, just stop hurting for a little while till I can catch my breath and give another push and get it out and get on with my life, whatever that's supposed to mean: looking after the question mark for a while, that's one thing for sure, tending my little being of indeterminate gender, with bud of both between its legs, soon to be one or the other and me a mother, careful to watch my diet, getting enough of the right stuff for lots of healthy milk to feed its little pink bud of a mouth I can't wait to see smile. Which is the least I should be able to expect of it after all it's put me through. Boy, I didn't think it'd be this hard. I mean, I knew it wouldn't be easy. Of course. I'm not naive. At least, I never used to think I was naive. And I guess I'm not now, because if you realize you're naive then you're not, are you? Or is that just being naive? But when it first started growing, or rather, let me say, when I first knew it was growing, all I felt was excited about it. Not that I don't feel excited any more. I do. But anyway, I didn't figure it would take this much out of me.

Not that I regret it. Not that it would make any difference if I did regret it, since there's nothing to be done about it now: it's happened. I just hope everything turns out all right, although all right for what, I don't know, I can't say, "all right" usually just meaning "the way I want it" and maybe the way I want it wouldn't be what is actually, after all, in fact, all right. I just hope some good comes out of it. But whatever happens, it sure doesn't look like there'll be much help from the male side. Utterly freaked. Obviously wishing it wasn't happening. Oh yeah, sure—"I'll get used to the idea." Fat chance. Anyway, we're in it together for the time being, I guess—all three of us; though I wish number three would put in an appearance, now that it's altered my metabolism and made me stop drinking and smoking and got me eating healthily, for its sake, for Blackie's sake, for my sake, for all our sakes, I suppose, now that there are more of us than I thought there'd be, and things are more complicated than I thought they'd get, though anyone would—and I should—have known that things always get complicated, never stay simple, never what they were, what you remember, what you want, remembering things the way you want them, wanted them: unchanged and unchanging, expression fixed, the strand of hair exactly there, hint of per-fume at the nape, the song still playing, eye smiling, hand placed precisely so, shoulder inclined at just that angle, torso bent a bit to left, legs straight, body swaying slightly—details you hold in memory where they won't hold still, not the same nor having been the same, the present elusive and the past more so, never as you want it, which is simply her being her and you being you and no other one there to confuse the issue, no issue there to confuse the other, you or her, the one inside the other, she or I or both, neither seeing eye to eye nor being completely at odds, the one with the other, the mother-to-be and me still wanting her as memory held her: holding me and wanting me before all others, though sometimes after others, the possible other always near, waiting to come between us, coming between us without actually being there, by merely being possible and therefore perhaps being something other than the other, something instead within us—one or the other or both—that we don't see or won't admit to and that comes between us when we think we're united, making everything different from what we thought it was, what we remember it as, what it is.

"What is it?" asked Blackie.

"What's what?"

"With you," she said. "You're different."

"No different," I maintained. "Still me."

"Still you, all right. But different. Distant."

Which was true. Not that I wanted it to be. At least, not that I remember wanting it to be. But then, who am I to say? Just because I remember it being a certain way doesn't mean that it was that way, since this is, after all, only my account and therefore not reliable as absolute truth, even though I am being as truthful as I can be, which I hope is truthful enough, although truthful enough for what, I can't say, I don't know, though I hope I might someday, some probably distant day: distant, as I was that day, those days, distant without—as I remember it—wanting to be, although, since I was indeed distant, maybe I did want to be, because if you are a certain way about something you perhaps must somewhere want to be that way—or anyway, I certainly did, wanting to distance myself in spite of myself, in spite of my better instincts, in spite of my attempts to be present, which were earnest enough, if not wholehearted, which Blackie couldn't help but notice, noticing that I wasn't really present, which I wanted to be, not wanting to be distant, which I was.

"Distant? Me? In what way?"

"For one thing, by not looking at me when we talk. Look at me, wouldja?"

"I'm looking, I'm looking. Stop badgering."

"I'm not badgering. I'm trying to make contact. You're disappearing on me."

And I am. My mind wanders and I wander, away from her, from it, from the fear of breach birth, Caesarean birth, early birth, late birth, hard birth, easy birth, birth; from the fear of toxemia, vision problems, headaches, discharges, bleeding, abdominal pain, chills, fever, problems of pregnancy, pleasures of pregnancy, pregnancy; from the fears of gestation, conception, sex, attraction, feeling. I wander into books, out to hockey, down to the store, up to the lake, off to a movie, round to the pub, over to a friend's, back to the office, away from the house, inside myself, retreating to where it's safe, curling up and shrinking, reversing the process that's unfolding in Blackie, where the baby lurks, holding its secrets it stole from us, twenty-three from her and twenty-three from me, shuffling its forty-six-card deck and beginning to play its hand, though having no hands to speak of, nor mouth to speak with, nor much of anything except a biological instruction kit of double helixes, a set of chemical memories slowly being expressed in cells, tissues, organs, and systems, the race muttering to itself in physical terms, forming another one of itself there inside

Blackie, where—as far as I'm concerned—it has no business being, at least not now, not until I'm ready, not until I want it, not until I can face the diapers, the crying and screaming, the three a.m. feedings, the drooling, the dribbling, the crawling, the climbing, the drawing on walls, the destruction, disobedience, music lessons, sports equipment, special schooling, pre-teen dating, adolescent rebellion, car-borrowing, underage drinking, drugs, irresponsible sex, ingratitude, disrespect, departure, disappearance.

"Disappearing? What do you mean, disappearing? I clean the kitty litter, I wash the dishes, I make the breakfast, I—"

"That's not what I'm talking about."

"Well, what then?"

"It's your manner, your energy, your—. It's—. You—. I—. Jesus! You know what I mean! Stop being so infuriating!"

But I couldn't stop being infuriating, any more than she could stop being infuriated by me, and when she'd break into tears I'd try to conciliate, which just seemed to infuriate her all the more, and she'd say I mustn't love her much if my love couldn't extend to its own result, which I didn't think was fair, since it'd only been a little while and I was still in shock: I'd try to rally, I'd build some enthusiasm, I'd be able to do just fine as the nine months progressed, with all the activity and emotional upheaval they'd entail: the choice and purchase of a layette, the preparation of the nursery and adaptation of the rest of the house, the concern at every new physical sensation, the early fear of tubal pregnancy and the later one of miscarriage, especially in Blackie's case, since she'd miscarried once before, which was why, for her, the fear was actually early rather than later and persisted despite reassurances from all quarters—from doctors and nurses, from books and magazines—that one miscarriage did not predispose her to another, although each reassurance had attached to it the earnest advice that a woman who has miscarried once and who, during a subsequent pregnancy, experiences any bleeding beyond a slight spotting, should proceed immediately to the nearest hospital emergency ward, which information didn't ease her mind, but did prepare us so that we knew what to do around the ninth or tenth week, when she discovered, in the middle of the night, a flow of vaginal bleeding, and woke me to speed her through the pre-dawn streets to the hospital, where I paced the emergency-ward waiting room while she underwent care and testing and was finally released with the assurance that she was fine, there was no miscarriage, the blood— as would doubtless soon be confirmed by the lab report (and her doctor would inform her)—was almost certainly menstrual, a delayed period, she'd apparently not been pregnant at all; no, they were in no position to say why the initial urine test had been positive—these things weren't infallible, a fluke maybe, one in fifty thousand, but it sometimes happened, perhaps a lab error, a mix-up of some sort; certainly, it was a crushing blow, a terrible letdown, she should go home and rest, see her doctor as soon as possible.

We drove home through the bustling morning streets in silence.

19

I am driving Blackie back from the hospital, the baby between
us, securely belted in a car chair, Blackie chattering comfort-
ingly to it or to me, to both of us probably, about the nice,
warm, loving home we're going to, where Mommy and
Daddy will take care of everything and there will be nothing
to worry about and Baby will sleep and eat and play and grow,
and Daddy is panicking because the car is stuck in reverse,
which gear Daddy had used in leaving the last-in-the-row
parking spot he'd had on the street outside the hospital, only
now he's in traffic and backing up into the oncoming flow,
trying to work the gearshift into drive, where it won't go, trying to ease the accelerator, which has no effect on the car's
speed, trying to simultaneously shift and accelerate to see if
that makes any difference, which it doesn't, the car backing
slowly towards the oncoming stream, which remains at the
same distance, me alone in the car, seeing in the rear-view
mirror the same unchanging scene, the tall buildings in the
background staying the same distance away, the bit of road

construction a few blocks back remaining the same few blocks back, the advancing traffic still the same advancing traffic, the vehicles in front and beside keeping the same distance in front and beside, everything moving but nothing changing in relation to each other, me still facing ahead within the car, one eye on the road in front, in case the forward gear suddenly engages, the other on the rear-view mirror, to keep track of what's happening behind, where nothing is. Where nothing, I mean, is happening—at least externally, in terms of what can be seen on the street. No telling what's happening in the cars, where families could be forming, mothers sitting with newborn infants in securely belted car chairs, crooning reassuring tunes or cooing consolingly to Baby, to Daddy, to both, about the happy home they're going to, the warmth and love amid which Baby will sleep and eat and play and grow, unaware of the fact that Mommy and Daddy's marriage is disintegrating around them and around Baby, who lies in innocent sleep, perhaps in that very car over there to the left, a little ways back in the outside lane, Mommy making caustic remarks to Daddy about his driving and other inadequacies, Daddy taking it all silently, with a sour look etching its way into permanent place on his face, building up his own store of resentment with which to fuel the divorce proceedings, the wrangling over possession and visiting rights, while I pull a cord on the hood of my windbreaker and the cord breaks and the strands of string that compose it unravel and I finger the strands thoughtfully, reflecting that I knew the cord was frayed, the strands ready to break, wondering if I could have prevented the final rupture by taking some measures to strengthen the bond while we were still of one accord, pregnant together or thinking we were, which amounts to about the same thing, at least in certain regards, united in anticipation of the imminent birth, she with enthusiasm, me with mounting dread, though the thought of desertion never so much as crossed my mind: the mere idea of her even thinking of leaving would have been more than I could bear, though in time, of course, I would be able to handle it, just as I would've been able to handle parenthood as the nine months progressed, if the nine months progressed, had the nine months progressed, which would have meant I wouldn't be alone in the car but would have Blackie and the baby there, the baby gurgling and squirming and crying and Blackie soothing it, soothing me, soothing both of us, all of us stock-still moving in the press of traffic on the afternoon street, the car's transmission jammed in reverse and me unable to correct the situation, Blackie becoming impatient with me about that, I think, unless I simply imagine her becoming impatient with me, when it is I, in fact, who am impatient with myself, stuck stalled moving, alone in a car with an inoperative drive gear and a world in neutral, where a mommy sits in a car crying over a daddy who doesn't want a baby who will squirm and gurgle and cry about the cord that's broken, feeling overwhelmed, empty, helpless, abandoned, trying to cope with being alone, at loose ends, fingering reflectively the unravelled strands of a cord we have to figure out what to do with—or, more exactly, without, for we have to admit it's irreparable. That much is clear. We know there's no going back, though I feel I can't go on and wonder if I could have prevented the final rupture by taking some measures to strengthen the bond after we learned that we hadn't been pregnant, after her doctor confirmed the diagnosis given at the hospital, encouraging her to keep trying: she was healthy and fertile and would yet become pregnant—a remark she reported to me rather pointedly, I thought, sensing her studying my features while awaiting my response, which was a noncommittal "Oh," uttered with stolid countenance and downcast eyes, for, as much as I wanted us to be in accord, I couldn't pretend, wouldn't if I could, no matter how much I wanted to reach out to her across the gap widening between us over deeper and deeper silences, knowing that the only way to do so was to lie, which I don't do, or which, at least, I try not to do, or anyway, would prefer not to do if I do do, which I may, not that I mean to, but which anyway, if I had done, would not really have been reaching out at all, the only way to reach out to her being to want to have a baby with her, which I wanted to want to do but which remained only the desire for a desire, a mere shadow where she wanted substance.

It smells like a hospital in here for some reason, that sharp, unpleasant, medicinal odour of—I don't know—formaldehyde or isopropyl alcohol or disinfectant or whatever the chemicals are whose aromas conspire to create the pungent, aseptic bouquets that perfume the air in those institutions that house the contradictory states of illness and recovery, healing and decay, pain and relief, birth and death. It smells like a hospital in here, though no material source of such odour is present in the place: I am without the basic rudiments of a first-aid kit, not even a band-aid, much as I keep reminding myself I should have some on hand. So the smell derives, I suppose, not from the physical environment but the mental one, arising from that place in memory where part of me still resides; in memory, where all of this resides; in memory, where I stand amid the hospital smells, realizing my utter inadequacy in the face of Blackie's despair as she relays the news that will cause her to have, through the ensuing months, a depression of post-partum proportions, a depression I witnessed with mute dismay, unable to manufacture the will to be a parent, and hence unable to console her in any real way, the only real way to console her being to will to be a parent, which I wouldn't, couldn't, didn't, wanting her but not wanting her pregnant, which was the only way she wanted me to want her, each of us wanting the other, but wanting the other another way, which maybe is just another way of wanting another, some other, some other or no other, other unchanging, as no other is, everything changing, changed from the past, in the present, in memory, which I write out, recovering, wondering if I've recounted things truthfully and accurately, or at least, truthfully and accurately enough, though truthfully and accurately enough for what, I'm not sure: for me, I guess; for memory, which is a way of holding, my only way of holding her now, with love or the memory of love, which I guess is a kind of imperfect love, which all love probably is, or at least mine is, or was, or hers was, or both ours were, not that it really matters whose was or wasn't, imperfect love or simply lust, which I was lost in, lost in lust and lost in her, lost in her and lost without her, lost before and after loss, an absence within me her presence made me feel, feeling some other, older loss or absence, vague in form and substance, which stirred obscurely within me, igniting ambiguous flames of fear and desire that shot through my veins and along my nerves—a weakening of the knees, a drop of the stomach, a loss of concentration on any and all but the one whose arch and supple feminacy distracted me from the terror that tore at me, that struck and withdrew, unnamed and unnameable, sinking back in seclusion somewhere within me, erupting again in anonymous flash, to once more retreat, just out of reach of mind or memory, with both of which I grope for understanding in the middle of the night, prodded awake by the dark, unspeaking, unspeakable dread that echoes dully and barely perceptibly deep in my gut and my unsettled brain, hovering darkly in the darkened room where I lie or sit on my bed in stunned apprehension, struggling to grasp the fleeting spectre of thought or experience, memory or dream, whatever it was, whatever it is that inspires this stark, uncomprehending fear. Each time it recurs, which is frequently now, its potency and opacity are equal to the time before, transfixing me anew in a high beam of panic that gradually subsides to consternation, concern, discomfort, puzzlement, placidity, the calm lasting a day perhaps, a week, a month, when another strike occurs, fresh in its impact and just as inchoate in content.

It is no longer transmutable, as, I realize now, it once was, so countless many times before Blackie and, for a while, with her, no longer transmutable, at the first inexplicable shot of adrenalin, into all-consuming, self-defeating, self-destructive obsessions with young and beautiful women, to whom I would gravitate, with instinct blind and unerring, time after unending time, spiralling into senseless fascinations, futile fallings-in-love, hopeless hangings-of-the-heart upon patently unobtainable objects of affection, or more properly, lust, passion, perversion, around whom I would orbit aimlessly and vainly, lost in them and to myself, as I had been lost in Blackie, until the night I found myself sunk sobbing to the floor, clutching at the carpet I crawled across, staring into the blank air, realizing something within me that was not love or lust, or passion, or perversion, but that clawed and struck like a living thing that was consuming me, defeating me, destroying me, and that I could not, cannot comprehend or name or know. There was a time I would have called it "not having her," whichever her I was then hung up on. But Blackie's changed that—or I have, because of Blackie; or perhaps in spite of her: because as long as she was there before me, unattainably, or there beside me, loving me, she masked it or shielded me from it. Or possibly her love strengthened me to face it, whatever it is, if it ever will take shape and come forth, which I feel it must and fear it will, torn as I am between desire and terror, stuck standing still, trying to look back and ahead simultaneously, to move forward, into or out of memory, striving to either remember or realize something that is not a mental image but a bodily phenomenon, a physical fact or feeling, whether sprung from the past or the present I don't know, I can't say, knowing only that it lies coiled somewhere within me, and that it now and again will lash violently, fleetingly out, suffusing my being with a paralyzing flush of alarm I somehow endure, clutching at reason and hope like tufts of the rug I clutched at in my horror and despair the night Blackie left that party with some other man, leaving me as perhaps some other once did, some other forgotten, some other forgetting, some other whose absence is present within me, some presence or absence sunk in seclusion somewhere just out of reach of mind or memory, all the more powerful for being so obscure, so elusive. If I could only know it, name it, encounter it long enough to take the measure of it, learn its contours, sense its purpose, I could maybe then find some peace, find my way back to Blackie or on to someone else. But I feel like I'm trying to map lightning, when lightning itself is my sole source of illumination. My only chance to locate it is when it strikes, but I can never know when it will, and when it does, can't get my eyes on it anyway, nor tell much about what its brief light reveals of anything it falls on.

◆ ◆ ◆

There's not much here except the furniture that's been left—or maybe I should say abandoned—by the folks I'm looking after this place for. They're not sure when they're coming back and I'm not sure how long I'm staying. The idea was to get out of town for a while, sort myself out some, escape the corporate hellhole I'd sunk into, try to sense a new direction for myself, maybe even make some plans, which—except for the plans—I guess is what's happening.

I didn't intend to write all this. There was a bunch of paper here and I just got started and wound up with this, whatever it is. And whatever it is, it's about all I've got right now, everything else gone into storage, except my clothes, of course, and a favourite painting by Blackie. It's got one of her trademark features, a combination of abstract and figurative elements. At the bottom of this large canvas, about five feet high by three or so across, there's a depiction of a sort of generic muscle structure that's somewhat reminiscent of the lower back, but without skin, like it might be in an anatomy book, and all rough and raw and vulnerable-looking, larger than life and done with great glopping cords of red and white and pink paint. Then this muscle structure separates and veers off to either side of the canvas, ascending gradually out towards the sides, like some kind of giant sinewy *v*, as if the two sides of the back were ripped apart, only there's not any kind of anatomical precision in the rendering, no identifiable muscles and no transition into arms or anything like that: just this independent muscle mass all twisting two ways up the canvas, with a sense of power and containment at the bottom, and attenuation and release at the top, where the two sides end. Enclosed within the sides, starting at the bottom, where the flesh begins to divide, a textured dome of black emerges, like the exposed crest of some dark element residing at the core of whatever or whoever this is, the black pigment ridged and rutted and almost sculpted, first striking the eye as abstract and irregular pattern, but gradually resolving, with extensive looking and play of mind, into subtle suggestions of human figures, whole and fragmented, depicted in extremes of exertion and emotion, writhing, contorted, tormented, agonized, striving, constrained, confined, as though trapped in some soul prison, racked with fury and despair. At its upper edges, the blackness gradually softens into lighter hues, which themselves evolve into brighter and stronger colours, reds and yellows and blues, fluttering and rippling and thrusting in a vibrant and exuberant kind of release, ascending the canvas and lifting forward from it in heavy and sensuous application of paint.

Sometimes when I'm sitting with it, I find it unsettling, even frightening, as though it were tapping into some universal primal terror—or maybe just telling me something about myself I don't want to know or remember; then another time I'll feel quite comforted by it, hopeful and uplifted, almost ecstatic. It's a lot like sex, I guess: desperate and thrilling and puzzling and pleasurable, physical and spiritual and mystic, all at the same time, or all at different times. Or at least that's what it seemed like for me with Blackie, which is maybe why I keep coming back to this painting so much, because it somehow conveys the feeling of what we had together, or could have had together, might have together or with another, I hope, sometime.

Blackie's signature's there in the lower right-hand corner as usual, the distinct if undecipherable squiggle of her surname, followed by the year the painting was done. On the back, she signed it more personally: "For Spenser. Love, Joanne."